JAX JILLIAN

Cover Design and Formatting
By Drue Hoffman, DRC Promotions

Edited by Stephanie Halliman-Garrett

PRAISE FOR LARKIN'S LETTERS

"It is an absolutely elegantly written story. This exquisitely written debut novel is one you should not pass up." – *Drue Hoffman, DRC Promotions*

"This book was phenomenal, and probably one of the best of this genre I have read in a long time" – *Kayla West, Journey with Books*

"*Larkin's Letters* is a must-read and should be on every person's reading list." – *Teri Lloyd, Sportochick's Musings*

"There are no words to say how much this book touched me. Great job and I look forward to reading more stories from this author." – *Deborah Bean, DRC Promotions Review Team*

"This superbly written debut novel is one you should not pass up, even with the sadness it makes you feel." – *Lynn Barret, Sassy Southern Book Affair*

"The author's skill at reaching my emotions and keeping me engaged guarantees I will pick up the next book I find with Jax Jillian's name." – *Laura Roth, Laura's Interests*

DEDICATION

For my baby son, Ryan. As you grow through life, may you find true love, catch it, hold onto it, nurture it, and never let it go.

ACKNOWLEDGEMENTS

Thank you to my family for supporting me as I embark on this new journey in my life. Your encouragement and love has only made me stronger and has helped me believe that you can do anything if you put your mind to it.

A special thanks to my "test readers": Ashley Grubb, Rachel Landgrebe, and Colleen Shahinian. Your input was valuable as I tried to make *Larkin's Letters* the best it could possibly be.

PROLOGUE

The brisk morning air pushed through the screen of the half-opened window. The sun burned through the thin curtains, and the warmth of the rays brushed upon his cheek as he opened his tired eyes. Her ocean-blue eyes stared back at him as he held her close. Her face was a calming sight, and he felt as if all was right with the world as long as she was close to him. She placed her hand on his face as he kissed her nose.

"Hey, blue-eyes." He kissed her forehead as he greeted her. "All I ask is that you give me today so I can prove to you that I'm your tomorrow."

"Hi, beautiful-faced boy," she responded, brushing his cheek with her fingers.

"I love you, Larkin," he whispered back.

"I left you something on the nightstand."

"You did? What is it?"

"Just turn over and look," she pleaded.

He turned over to look, hesitantly, not

wanting to look away from her. She always seemed to disappear every time he looked away. A manila envelope lay atop the white rustic nightstand and the word "Ryan" was penned across the front, beckoning him. He glared at the envelope for just a moment before turning back to her, but she was gone.

"Larkin? Larkin?" he desperately cried out for her. "Please, Larkin. Don't leave me. I'm not ready." He reached for the pillow that lay next to his head, intact and untouched for the past two months, and pulled it in close to him, craving her scent and yearning for her to come back to him.

CHAPTER 1

Ryan Boone sat on top of the lightning-white sand dune underneath the darkening sky as the sun was starting to set over the New Jersey shoreline. This was the first time he came to this spot since...since...well, he still couldn't believe what had happened. It was late March 2013, and there was a crisp, chilly breeze in the air. He should have brought a sweatshirt with him, he thought to himself. Wearing only khaki shorts, flip- flops, and a gray Harley Davidson T-shirt adorning his 6'2" muscular frame, he was still used to those warm and sunny California springs. The storm clouds were getting closer and closer. It's going to be a big one, he thought.

There were about a half-dozen shrieking seagulls circling overhead, but there was something refreshing about the sounds of their screams. It was a familiar sound, one he had grown accustomed to over the past year living here. Ryan threw out some pieces of bread for his old friends. "Sorry, I haven't been here in a while," he said.

He looked out into the surrounding unsettled Great Egg Harbor Bay and noticed it was empty. All the boats had docked due to the impending storm, but it was fitting. He didn't really want anyone around right now. All he wanted was just him and these letters he held in his pocket. As he grasped the envelope and pulled it out, he felt his hands shaking. Why was it so hard? Why couldn't he just open it? For the past year, he had been as strong as any man could be. But now, this envelope, this piece of paper, was breaking him down.

He stared at the sealed envelope for a moment before placing it back in his pocket. He noticed the corners had slightly folded over, and the blue ink that read "Ryan" on the front had faded a little bit. It had been two months since he got the letters, and it looked like they had been through a war, just like he had been for the past year and a half. They had been constantly in and out of his pocket every day with his every intention of opening them, but he had yet to. Every time he looked at them, he felt sick to his stomach. He began to think about how he got to this place in his life. The last two years had been the best years of his thirty- six-year-old life, but now he was in the darkest place he could ever imagine. He was in hell, he thought, and he couldn't imagine that a heaven even existed.

He slowly pulled the envelope out again and brought it to his nose, desperately trying to capture any familiar scent from it that would take him back to the happy times when he had never felt so alive.

As he brought it down from his face, he started to weep. This was the only thing he had left to hold on to, and he needed to somehow find the courage to open it. He thought about how strong she had been to write these letters, and he felt he owed it to her to be strong enough to read them.

Ryan gathered himself together as the storm clouds drew closer. The sky was darkening, and the hungry seagulls continued to circle overhead. He threw the last of the bread to them. "Sorry, guys, it's all I have left." The wind was starting to pick up, and it was biting at his face. The sand was circling around him with each gust. He needed a way to read these letters before the storm came in.

Ryan wiped his tears away from his misty eyes and slowly slid his finger underneath the sealed flap. He pulled the first letter out and took a deep breath as he began to unfold it. He glanced at the top of the page.

To my beautiful-faced boy,

As he read that first line, he began to weep again. After folding the letter back up, he returned it back into his pocket. He didn't understand how she expected him to do this. He wasn't strong enough yet, but he knew he needed to be. Just like she was.

As the storm clouds drew closer, lightning was flashing in the distance. Ryan closed his eyes and remembered the times they would dance in the rain. She would twirl her body around, looking up toward the angry sky with her hands in the air. She would drag him to their private beach, and they would dance chest to chest as the wet sand would bond to their bare feet. It was as if they were in their own little world, and nothing else mattered.

The distant thunder startled Ryan out of his memory, and he suddenly remembered why he was there. Larkin's letters. His hands trembling, he pulled out the letter again and began his journey. He didn't know where this journey was going to take him, and he could only hope these letters would take him to somewhere better than where he was now.

Letter #1 - March 3, 2011

To my beautiful-faced boy,

Ryan, my dearest Ryan, you always say to me that I am your favorite lullaby. But you know what? You are my favorite lullaby. I don't need music, and I don't need sound. I just need your arms around me, and I can sleep through any pain, any sorrow. You called me last night. You couldn't sleep. If only you had known that I couldn't sleep either, but I didn't say anything. You needed me, and I will do anything for you—my best friend.

As always, when you can't sleep, you call me, and I read to you my work in progress, my debut novel that I have been slaving over these past four months. You are the only one who has read, or I should say listened, to my manuscript. You are the only one who cares. You are the only one who believes in me. But of course you do. You're my best friend, and that is what best friends do. They believe in each other.

Ryan, you are probably wondering why I am writing to you. I have some news. Bad news. And as you know, I am better at writing my feelings down. I need to practice. I don't know how I am going to tell you, but maybe if I write it down, it'll give me the courage to tell you. I don't want to tell you on the phone. I want to tell you in person, but I don't know when I will see you again. When will I see you again, Ryan? God, I hope it is soon. I need my best friend. My lullaby.

My dearest Ryan, I have leukemia.

Ryan folded up the letter and placed it in the back of the letters that lay in the crinkled envelope. He had no idea. No idea that his childhood best friend, his wife, Larkin James, had been writing to him this whole time. The sky darkened, and rain started to fall. He quickly sheltered the envelope under his arm as he hurried back to the bay house that he and Larkin had shared.

He placed the envelope down on the kitchen counter next to the bouquet of flowers that had been delivered to him that morning, and he started to prepare a pot of coffee. Every morning since her death, a fresh bouquet of flowers was hand-delivered by Harry Wakefield, the owner of the corner flower shop up the street. She had arranged for Harry to deliver them to Ryan, and he had no idea for how long they would keep coming. Harry, for some reason, wouldn't tell him. Knowing Larkin, she had had it all planned out. Knowing Larkin, they would keep coming forever.

As the water noisily squirted through the filter into the pot, Ryan took notice of the pictures that were plastered on the refrigerator and the pictures that decorated the walls. Pictures of him and Larkin. Pictures of their wedding day. Pictures of them with her parents. Pictures of them with his best friends—Ian Marsico, Sarah Madison, and Jason Gray. While waiting for the coffee to finish, he pulled a photo album out of the top drawer of the end table in the living room that Larkin had put together about six months ago. There were so many pictures. *Thank God*, he thought. All he had left were pictures. Pictures of their life together starting all the way back to when they were kids living next door to each other in Somers Point, New Jersey.

His thoughts scattered as he maneuvered through the photos, and ultimately, his mind reverted back to the letters. Ian had explained to Ryan that Larkin had asked him to hold on to the letters and give them to him after she died. And Ryan had been unable to open them until now, two months later. He had only read the first one, and he had no idea how he was going to get through all of them. His pain was still fresh. He was mad at himself. He hated himself for what had happened. He had made her a promise, and he broke that promise. For that, he would never forgive himself.

The humming of the coffeepot had stopped,

and the sudden silence was ironically deafening, extracting Ryan out of the trance he had fallen into while looking at the pictures. He closed the album shut and entered back into the kitchen, and, as he prepared himself a cup, the envelope that had been sitting on the counter beckoned him while he endlessly stirred the sugar granules into the coffee. *I can't do it, Larkin. How do you expect me to do this? I'm not ready. Not yet.* He stared at the envelope until it became a white blur and the word "Ryan" had become out of focus. All he could think of was the first letter he had read and the memory it had unburied. He remembered that night he called her, but he had no idea. No idea that she had wanted to tell him then about her cancer.

Ryan reached for his left ring finger, but nothing was there. He always played with his wedding band. He wasn't used to the fact that it was no longer there. It was a cold, rainy night in New Orleans in early March 2011, and he was sitting on the balcony of his rented condo watching the rain and listening to the thunder as the lightning lit up the night sky. It was 2:00 a.m., and he was tired. He had just finished filming for the day and had to get up early for another long day of filming. But, unfortunately he couldn't sleep. Ever since the divorce, he had many sleepless nights. It had been six months, but he still wasn't quite over it yet. He never thought that he would be here at this point of his life: divorced at thirty-four. He never thought that his marriage would have only lasted for two years. He was not the ladies' man that the media made him out to be. He was a good man. He loved her, and he tried to make it work. She was the one who didn't try, but he didn't care what everyone else thought. He knew the truth about himself, and so did his family and closest friends.

The wind was picking up speed, and the rain was starting to blow sideways. As the puddles started to form on the balcony floor, Ryan made his way inside, slipped off his saturated flip-flops, and turned on the television. Even though he was a professional actor, he never seemed to be too interested in watching TV. He needed to find a way to get some sleep, and he thought maybe the TV, coupled with the sound of the rain thumping against the window, was enough to serenade him to sleep. But not this time. After tossing and turning for almost half an hour, he surrendered to his insomnia, reached for his phone, and made a call to the one person who knew him best, the one person who was always there for him. It was late, but he knew she would answer. She always did.

"Ryan? What's wrong?" she answered. The sound of her voice was so comforting, so pleasing, he couldn't help but smile.

"Hey, sweetie. I am so sorry it's late." He really was sorry that he woke her, but not sorry to hear her voice.

"No problem. Let me guess. You can't sleep?" It was amazing how well she knew him, he thought.

"No," he said with desperation in his voice.

"All right, hold on, okay?"

"Sure." He knew what he was holding on for.

Larkin James was Ryan's best friend since childhood. They grew up next door to each other, and they had been there for each other for everything, big or little. She was the one person he went to for anything because he knew she would always be there. She was the only one who encouraged him to follow his dream of being an actor when everyone else didn't, including his family. She made it to every single one of his movie premieres, and she was there at his wedding. She never missed anything that meant something to him. And she never missed one late-night phone call when he couldn't sleep.

"All right, you still there, Ryan?" she finally said after about three minutes of putting him on hold, but he didn't mind.

"Of course, I am still here." He would've held for her all night.

"Okay, I'll pick up where I left off last time, or where at least I think I left off before you fell asleep.

Larkin began to read to Ryan. She was reading him a novel that she was writing called *Jillian's Touch*. He was the only one that she would let listen to or read the manuscript, or at least that was what she had told him. In fact, she told him he was the only one who knew she was writing a book, well, except for her husband, and he was happy to listen. Like she always encouraged him to follow his dream, he reciprocated. He didn't only listen because he was her friend. He actually enjoyed the story she was reading to him. He thought it was amazing, and he couldn't wait for her to finish it so she could hopefully get it published. Larkin wasn't always the most optimistic person in the world, and she, of course, didn't think it was that good. But he insisted to her that it was.

"Is that why you fall asleep? Because it's so good?" she would ask him sarcastically.

"Of course not, Larkin. You know that. I wouldn't keep calling to hear it if it was bad, would I?" He would try to reassure her, and it was the truth. But most importantly, he would call because Larkin reading the book to him was like her singing him a lullaby.

> *Jillian led Nathan to the room that would change everything. She was shaking because she wasn't quite sure how he would react. But she knew she was doing the right thing. At least she hoped she was. As they turned the corner and entered the room, she felt him let go of her hand. She looked at his face and where there used to be a look of love and happiness was now a look of horror and desperation.*

The familiarity of her voice always brought him back to his childhood where the two of them were inseparable. They shared some great times growing up, but their career choices—well, mainly his career choice—would eventually break that inseparability, but no matter what, they were still the best of friends.

The screaming of the alarm clock violently awoke Ryan. As he battled through the cloudiness that the sleep had left in his mind, that was the last thing he remembered hearing last night before dozing off. He knew Larkin would help him fall asleep. It's almost as if he was looking forward to another sleepless night so he could call her and listen to more of her story. He thought she was a great writer. He always felt bad falling asleep while she read to him, but he knew she understood and was always willing to help him. So like every other morning after she read to him the night before, he sent her a text message thanking her.

> *Hey, Blue Eyes. Thanks for last night. As always, you're my favorite lullaby. Can't wait to hear what happens in the room where Jillian took Nathan. Talk to you soon. Love, Fish.*

CHAPTER 2

Letter #2 - March 11, 2011

Dear Ryan,

I decided I am going to tell you everything in these letters. Everything. Every last detail. Quotes from our conversations. Quotes from conversations I have with other people. That way, you can remember everything we share and be a part of everything that we don't get to share.

I spent the evening sitting on the front porch on this unusually warm March night. I didn't even need to put on a sweatshirt. The porch swing was still slightly damp from the earlier rainstorm, and there was still a mist in the air, but the clouds had started to break. I often sit out there at night after a long day at work. I need the peace and quiet which is a far cry from the hustle and bustle of my job. It's kind of ironic, though. Most people wouldn't associate living in the city, especially a big city like Philadelphia, as peaceful and quiet. But Chris and I are lucky. Lucky that we live in a small neighborhood nestled away in a corner of the city that is calm and inviting. Not too much traffic and all our neighbors help each other out. St. Patrick's Day is only a few days away, and most of my neighbors have flashing white-and-green shamrock-shaped lights outlining the edges of their roofs and windows, and toy leprechauns are dancing in the front yards.

How's the weather in New Orleans? I am sure it is a little bit warmer there. We just got walloped by a Nor'easter four days ago which has become somewhat of a weekly occurrence these days in Philadelphia. It is nice though to see the barren tree branches start to thaw out and small patches of grass start to emerge from underneath their white winter coat.

I had a conversation with Chris tonight. I do love him so much, but he just doesn't seem to believe in me the way you do. I told him I was almost done with my manuscript, and I needed to try to find someone who was willing to publish it. He just rolled his eyes and begged me to not get my hopes up. I told him you believed in me and think I have a shot. Unfortunately, he thinks you live in a completely different world than we do. He thinks everything comes easy for you and that if you just snap your fingers you'll get what you want. He doesn't know you, Ryan. Not like I do. He doesn't know how hard you worked to become one of the most sought-after actors in Hollywood. He doesn't know what you gave up and how you struggled to make ends meet when you first moved to Los Angeles at the age of nineteen. He doesn't understand our bond, and I don't think he ever will. He is a hard man, Ryan, much different from you. He is a hardworking man, and I know he would do anything to provide for me, but sometimes I just need my best friend. I need you.

I still haven't told Chris that I have leukemia. I know, I know. I know what you're thinking. But how can I? How do you tell your husband that you are dying? It's not an "oh, by the way" type of conversation. "Hey, honey, we're out of milk, I'm going to the store. Oh, by the way, I have leukemia. See you when I get home." I don't know, Ryan. How do I tell him? I wish you were here to help me. But then again, I haven't even told you yet. As if the question of "how do I tell him?" isn't hard enough. How do I tell you, Ryan?

I often find myself drifting back to our childhood together. We were lucky, Ryan. We grew up in a playground. The beach, the boardwalk, the water, the fishing, the amusement rides. What more could you ask for growing up? I fondly remember you being my protector. You always looked out for me. You were like a big brother to me. The brother I never had. The sister you never had. But it was so much more than that. You were my best friend. You taught me everything. Well, it seems like everything. My favorite memories were going out on your father's boat on the Great Egg Harbor Bay, and, as you fished, I would read to you. I looked forward to every Saturday and our time fishing together on the pier. You were the only person I could tell my dreams to, and I, in turn, couldn't wait to see if the dreams that you confided in me came true. And they did, Ryan. Your dreams came true. And it makes me believe that mine can too. At least, I used to. But now, this. Leukemia. If that word doesn't wake you up right out of your dreams, then I don't know what word would.

I never believed I was good enough. You would spend countless hours telling me that my writing was good enough, and I was special and could do anything. Why were you so good to me, Ryan? Why?

I don't know if you know this, but when we would go out on your father's boat, I would just sit and watch you as you fished. As you baited and casted the line. As the intricately defined muscles in your arm would bulge as you would frantically pull on the line when you felt it jump and reel in the catch. As you carefully unhooked the fish and measured it to see if it was a keeper. You were perfect in every way, Ryan. I always thought you were a beautiful man. I just never had the courage to tell you.

You taught me more than just how to fish. Do you remember when you taught me how to surf, how to ride a boogie board, how to Jet Ski and water ski? You were my fish. I miss you, Fish. You helped me conquer my fear of water. And I'll never forget the time when I was sixteen and you were seventeen and our Jet Ski sunk and we were stranded in the middle of the inlet under the

Longport Bridge that hovered over the bay. You promised me everything would be okay, and you wouldn't let anything happen to me. We had our life jackets on, but I was still scared and you knew it. You never let go of me until help came. I need you to hold on to me again, Ryan. I'm scared again, and you always know what to do.

God, he missed her. He missed everything about her. The way she smiled. The way she smelled. The way she looked at him with her crystal clear blue eyes. He missed the way her bangs swept across her forehead. The way she would hold his hand as they would walk along the beach where the water met the sand. He missed the times she would walk out just beyond their deck and carve "Ryan + Larkin forever" inside a giant heart in the sand. The times when her face would light up every morning when he brought her a fresh bouquet of flowers. He missed the way she made him feel. He missed her strength and her courage. He missed the time that had been erased because it took him almost a decade to realize his love for her.

He missed their childhood, too. Her letter brought him back, and it was as if he was reliving it all over again. Larkin probably didn't realize it, but it wasn't just him doing all the teaching. He learned things, too. It was Larkin who taught him how to dance. The month before his junior prom, Larkin would come over every day and dance with him in his room, and she taught him patience. She was so patient with him and his two left feet, but she never gave up on him and he finally got the hang of it.

She also helped him get over his fear of heights. After three summers of trying, she finally convinced him to go parasailing with her the summer after his senior year, and he was glad he did. It was one of the best experiences of his life. Even though they were the best of friends, they fought like brother and sister. Larkin was always quick to tell Ryan when she thought he was being a jerk, whether it was toward a girl or his family, and he was always quick to tell her to butt out. No matter how bad their arguments got, they would always laugh about it later on the phone before they fell asleep.

She had never dated a whole lot while they were in school. She did have one or two boyfriends but nothing very serious. She focused on her studies, and she was very athletic, playing practically every sport. She was very shy, and she had a small group of friends, many of them being her teammates. He, on the other hand, was very outgoing and had a lot of friends. He was the class clown, and there weren't many kids who didn't like him. And all the girls liked him. He was voted "Best Looking" and "Most Likely to be Famous" in his senior year. Even though he had several girlfriends throughout high school, not one of those relationships was as special to him as his friendship with Larkin. Many of his friends would ask him why he didn't date Larkin. As close as they were, they never even came close to dating. He remembered talking to her about it one day when they were fishing.

"What do you make of all these people saying we should date?" he had asked her.

"I don't know, Ryan," she answered. "I guess I never really thought about it. Have you?"

"I don't know. I guess I think about it when someone asks me about it."

"I mean," she started to say, "it's not that I wouldn't date you, but you are my best friend. I think dating each other would ruin that. I would rather have you as my best friend than take the chance to not have you in my life because we end up hating each other."

"I agree," he said. And he did agree. Although he did think she was beautiful, and he certainly would ask her out if he had just met her on the street yesterday. He would never do anything to compromise their friendship.

Two letters down. How many more to go? He had no idea. He wanted to get through this. He needed to read these letters. She had left them for him, and he owed it to her to read them. He finished his coffee and placed the mug in the sink. He noticed it was getting late. He hadn't been able to sleep well, and the thought crossed his mind that maybe Larkin could help him get some sleep. After all, she would read to him when he wasn't able to. Maybe she couldn't read to him now, but he could read her letters and that would be just as good, right?

He retired to his bedroom and changed into a white tank top and a pair of plaid boxer shorts. He climbed into his king-sized bed that laid out before a set of French doors which opened up into a small second floor balcony. He and Larkin had spent many nights sitting on that balcony, talking about their future and her sickness. He would give anything to have those nights back. Anything.

Letter #3 - April 20, 2011

Hey, Fish,

It's been over a month since I last wrote to you. It's been pretty hectic around here. I lost my job, Ryan. The hospital underwent a series of layoffs, and my department was the hardest hit. I found out two weeks ago. The horrible part about it is I am supposed to start chemotherapy next month, and now I can't. No job equals no health insurance. What am I to do, Ryan? I am so scared, and I really don't know what to do. I can't call you because I still haven't told you yet. I need to tell you.

It's been an awful two weeks. Chris and I have separated. When I lost my job, I told him I didn't want to find another one. I wanted to focus on my writing. He didn't quite see eye-to-eye with me on that one. He begged me to reconsider my decision. I know I should find a new job, but who is going to hire someone who has leukemia and is dying? I know the smart thing to do is to find a new job and get health insurance, but, Ryan, I want to write. Especially now, when my time may be limited. Why can't he see that? Why can't he support me on that?

I know you are probably wondering why I don't just add myself to Chris' health insurance policy. Well, I still haven't told him I am sick. He doesn't know. I was going to tell him, but, when I saw how he reacted to my wanting to write full time, I knew he would have only stayed with me out of guilt. I don't want that. If it is that easy for him to just walk away from me, then his love for me isn't as strong as I had thought, and I am better off alone.

I now know how you felt when you and Abigail got divorced. You would tell me how alone and down you felt. That all your sacrifices meant nothing. You'll never admit it to me, but I know how hurt you must have been by the media and the public's portrayal of you as a ladies' man, claiming you had cheated on her. But you do not need to worry because I know the truth, your family knows the truth, and your friends know the truth. I want you to understand that, Ryan. Understand that we know the truth. We know what kind of man you are. You are a good man, a generous man, a man who would never turn his back on someone he loves. And I know how much you loved her. I could tell from the very first minute you introduced me to her at your father's funeral. You never left her side, Ryan, and you never let go of her hand. Not even when I got there. That was the first time you put another girl first before me, and I will admit I missed you needing me, but I was happy you were happy, and that's all I cared about. I wasn't surprised when you told me you were marrying her six months later. She was beautiful, Ryan. The type of beautiful that makes every other woman jealous. You tried to make it work. I know you did. You both were just too busy working, and, unfortunately, work seems to take precedence over love these days.

I feel like that with Chris. He used to never let go of my hand when we would go for a walk or when we would watch a movie together, but then the walks and the movies started becoming few and far between, and ultimately, so did the hand holding. So did the playful glances and flirting. Instead, what became more important was working so we could pay the bills. The little things were put on the back burner, and ultimately, that flame eventually burned out.

That's not the way it should be, right? The flame should never burn out. Why does it have to? Because of bills and responsibilities that need to be taken care of? I still believe in love, Ryan. I still believe in those long walks on the beach and sharing a bowl of ice cream and having a man wrap his arms around mine while helping me to reel in a big catch. I still believe in lying next to each other on the hood of the car at the drive-in movie theater. I believe in a man opening the door for me and pulling my chair out for me before I sit down to eat dinner at an intimate, fancy restaurant. I believe in flowers and all that they symbolize, and I believe in always kissing good night before going to sleep. I believe in falling asleep every night in the arms of the man that I love, and I want a man to believe in me. Believe in all that I can give him because I want to give a man everything I am. Most importantly, I want someone to be proud of me.

But now I don't know, Ryan. I don't know if I will ever get to experience it again. My time is limited, and I have no idea what the future holds for me.

One thing I do know, Ryan, is that I miss you. Did I ever tell you that the day you left for Los Angeles when you were nineteen, I cried for hours? I did. I cried and cried and cried. I never let you see me cry though. I still had senior year to get through, and I had no idea how I was going to do it without you. My fish. My best friend. But I was so proud of you. I am proud of you and how successful you have become, but you never did really leave me behind. You were always there for me, and you never forgot me. You easily could have. You have traveled the world filming movies, meeting new people, and experiencing new adventures. You could have easily forgotten me.

I want to thank you, Ryan. Thank you for not leaving me behind. Thank you for making it to my high school and college graduations. Thank you for coming to my high school basketball state championship game. Thank you for never forgetting a birthday or an anniversary. Thank you for taking me to your big movie premieres. Thank you for being you. Thank you for being my best friend. Thank you for being so good to me.

Letter #4 - May 9, 2011

Ryan,

It's been a couple of weeks since I last wrote. I still haven't told you yet. It haunts me. Why am I so afraid of the one person who will protect me? I have been thinking a lot about time lately. You used to say to me, "Larkin, life is all about timing." It didn't really dawn on me how true that is until the past couple of months. Time. Not a big word. But it is definitely a big concept. When you look up the word "time" in the dictionary, it gives you several definitions including: a period with limits, a moment something occurs, an interval, a minute or hour, one's lifespan. On the other hand, when you look up "timeless" in the dictionary, you find it to mean unchanged, eternal, undying, and ageless. Over the past two months, I have thought more and more about time. It isn't something you really think about unless you or someone you love is dying.

Do you think time can be timeless? Anyone you ask would probably say no. I would have said the same thing, but these past couple of months, I have tried my hardest to turn the answer to that question into a yes. After all, love can become loveless. Sensibility can become senseless. Morality can become virtueless. So then, why not? Why can't time become timeless? It's a long shot, I know. I guess that is why we have memories. Our memories are what make time timeless, don't you think? I think time is something everyone takes for granted.

It is a gift, a privilege. Time is something we should nurture and care for like it is our child. Time isn't just how it is defined above. It is also, most importantly, the best medicine we could ever have. As you continue to read these letters, and from here on after, I want you to remember one thing: time heals what reason cannot.

The rain was pounding against the bedroom window, and the thunder stirred Ryan from his sleep. As his weary eyes adjusted to the darkness, he could feel her arms wrapped around his chest. He could feel her breathing, and he pressed his nose against the top of her head, taking in the lavender scent from her hair.

"Larkin…wake up. Larkin…" He raised her chin up to bring her eyes level to his.

"Hey, beautiful," she whispered to him.

"God, you look like an angel." He pulled her closer to him and pressed his lips against hers.

"Don't leave me this time." He pleaded with her.

She grabbed his face with her hands. "I will never leave you, Ryan. I am always here with you."

"I love you so much, Larkin."

"I love you too." She stroked the back of his head as his tears began to release from his exhausted eyes. "I left you something in the drawer of the nightstand."

"No." He swiftly rotated his neck from one shoulder to the other. "No. I am not looking. Every time I look away, you're gone. Not this time. You can't leave. I am not ready to let you go. Not yet."

"Yes, you are, Ryan. I won't leave you. I will always be here." She wiped a tear away from his cheek. "It's time, Ryan. Close your eyes."

"No, I won't. I want to see you. I need to see you."

"Close your eyes. I'm right here." She placed his face in her hands. "Close your eyes and kiss me."

He pulled her face to his, closed his eyes, and joined his lips with hers. He breathed as much of her in as he could. As he felt her pull away from their embrace, he opened his eyes. She was gone. Her absence took his breath away, and, as he tried to catch his breath, his chest was squeezing his heart so tight, he swore it was breaking. He sat up, rested his forehead in his hands, and began to weep. He was sure he wasn't ready to let her go. He was sure he never would be. He was sure he couldn't live without her.

He had wanted to keep reading her letters last night, but they weren't helping him. The letters were too personal. They were just conjuring up memories of her. Memories of them together. The memories were what kept him awake. He needed her voice. He needed to feel her.

He looked over at the nightstand to check the time. It was 3:30 a.m. It was still pitch-black outside, and the thunder echoed off of the bay, rattling the pictures on the wall with each rumble. Sleep was his enemy right now. As much as he wanted to dream of her and wake up with her in his arms, he couldn't bear to feel her slip away from his grasp every time he realized she wasn't real. But he couldn't go back to the letters. He needed to escape from them. Instead, he thought maybe a book was just what he needed. He went to his nightstand to grab the novel *Indignation.* He had started it several months ago but never finished it because—well— because there were more important things to deal with at the time. As he opened the nightstand drawer, he couldn't believe what he saw. He noticed his watch lying on top of Larkin's manuscript, *Jillian's Touch.* She had never finished reading it to him. And his watch. He had wondered what happened to it. He had taken it off when he took a leave of absence from acting because he didn't want to be reminded of all it had meant to him. He had forgotten about it, and when he did think about it, he couldn't bear to put it back on. Besides, he hadn't been able to find it. As he picked up the watch and her manuscript, he shook his head in disbelief. There was a small note paper clipped to the front.

Remember, time heals what reason cannot. It's time, Ryan.

He removed the note from on top of the manuscript and noticed the cover page.

Jillian's   Touch.   Screenplay   by   Larkin James.

He couldn't believe it. *When did she do that?* he thought to himself. She had always said that she was going to write him the role of his lifetime. He had no idea, but she had started to adapt her manuscript into a screenplay. She always had a way of bringing things together, he thought to himself. She had planted the watch and the unfinished screenplay there. She knew that was where he kept *Indignation* and he would eventually open that drawer to finish reading it. She also knew he couldn't read when his mind wasn't clear. That's why he stopped reading it to begin with. He couldn't focus. He knew that she knew when the time came for him to open that drawer to read, he was ready. Ready to get back to who he really was. That's why she came to him. To guide him toward that drawer.

Larkin's last letter about time struck a chord with Ryan. That, coupled with her ghost, the note that was clipped to the manuscript, and the watch. They were enough to summon another memory. A small memory. An insignificant memory, but, nevertheless, another memory.

Ryan glanced at the watch on his left wrist to check the time. The time was 8:04 p.m. It had been five months since that March night Larkin had read to him, and, although they tried to talk at least once a week since, he hadn't made any late-night calls. *Where has the time gone?* he asked himself. Larkin hadn't left his mind since two nights ago when his mom called him to ask if he had spoken to her lately. Unfortunately, he hadn't spoken to her in about three weeks. He had been in South Africa filming, so their time difference was six hours, and it was hard to coordinate a time to talk between their bouncing up and down. He was sure it sounded like a beaver chucking wood as he chewed each and every one of his fingernails. His plane was scheduled to touch down at 8:30 p.m., but, as the minute hand on the watch kept creeping and creeping toward the six, the knot in his stomach was getting tighter and tighter. As the plane descended into Philadelphia, Ryan watched through the window as the city skyline grew bigger and bigger. And as he thought about what he was possibly going to say to Larkin, he was startled by a strange voice.

"That's a nice watch you got there," said the man sitting next to him. He looked over at the strange man. He was probably in his sixties, Ryan thought. He certainly dressed like he was, that's for sure. He had a paisley shirt adorned with a striped wide tie, and he could see brown trouser straps peeking out from behind his plaid, collarless jacket. He seemed harmless enough, so Ryan acknowledged his compliment.

"Oh, thanks. It was a gift." Larkin had given him that watch the night before he won the award for best actor one year ago.

"Well, that's a pretty nice gift. Do you mind if I take a look at it?" Ryan thought this was a strange request, but he obliged and handed over the black and navy-blue watch. He figured the man probably saw how nervous he was acting, and he was probably just trying to make small talk to help calm his nerves.

"Ah, an *Invicta*. These are great watches."

He was sure the man sitting next to him was considerably annoyed. Ryan couldn't stop his knee from bouncing up and down.

"Do you know a lot about watches?" Ryan asked, trying to be polite. The last thing he wanted to do right now was talk to a stranger about watches.

"Yes, probably more than the average person. I'm a jeweler, and I often work on watches too."

As the man examined it, Ryan could see his interest was piqued at the back of the watch. The man read aloud the inscription on the back. "*Your acting is timeless.* You an actor?" he asked seemingly surprised.

Ryan was thrilled the man didn't know who he was. "Yes, yes, I am." Sometimes he thought it would just be easier to say no, but he never could bring himself to lie.

"Really!? That's pretty interesting! Forgive me if I should recognize you, but I am not a big movie person."

"No, no forgiveness needed. It's quite all right. Really."

"I was wondering why everyone kept looking back here. I thought maybe there was something wrong with me, but now I know they were looking at you," the man said as he chuckled. "Well, you must be pretty talented if all these people know who you are."

"I don't know about that," replied Ryan. Despite his fame and good looks, he was a very humble man.

"Well, whoever got you this watch must think your acting is pretty special," said the man as he handed the watch back to Ryan. While his hands trembled, he struggled to put the watch back on. He was so shaky; Ryan figured the man probably thought he was on something.

As the plane landed and taxied to the terminal, Ryan shook the stranger's hand. "It was a pleasure talking with you, sir."

"Likewise, I'll be sure to look you up and check out one of your movies. What's your name?"

"Ryan, Ryan Boone. Thanks, I appreciate that."

Ryan weaved his way through the airport terminal with his head down like a raging bull. He was in a hurry, and he didn't want anyone to recognize him. He wasn't in the mood for admirers. As he entered into baggage claim, he again checked the time. It was 8:45 p.m. He grabbed his bag off the baggage belt, hailed a cab, and started the last leg of his almost twenty-four-hour journey to see Larkin. She didn't know he was coming, and he still didn't know what he was going to say to her. He only knew he had to be there for her, like she had always been for him.

It was 9:17 p.m. when the cab pulled up to the hotel. It was an oppressive August evening in Philadelphia, and the darkness of the night cast an unusual eeriness in Ryan's gut. He couldn't quite understand this feeling he was having. He was anxious to see Larkin, but, at the same time, he didn't know what to expect when he saw her. She didn't know that he knew, and he still didn't know what he was going to say. He didn't know if he was more angry at her for her not telling him herself, or if he was more frightened at what was to come next. The cab dropped Ryan off at the front entrance of the hotel. It was a nice hotel, not like the luxury hotels he normally stayed at, but it was nice. It was your average hotel with red and black checkered carpets and lavish crystal chandeliers hanging every five yards from the cathedral ceiling. As he entered through the lobby, he noticed a bar with about a half dozen people to his right, and the check-in desk was to his left. Thankfully, his mom had told him Larkin's room number so he didn't have to waste any time trying to get that information from the staff. The elevators were just past the check-in desk, and he made sure to not make eye contact with anyone as he passed by. It felt like an eternity waiting for the elevator door to open, and, as it finally did, he was relieved to see no one else got on it with him. The doors opened up on the fourth floor, and Ryan purposely took his time walking to her room. He studied each room number on the doors as he passed by, and, as the numbers kept getting closer and closer to hers, he could feel his breaths getting shallower and shallower. He had never been so scared before in his life, but he needed to be strong. He knew Larkin was going to need him. He had spent the past decade playing all sorts of roles, but he realized this was going to be the biggest role of his life. This was reality. No awards will be given out for this performance.

That night. That hot, oppressive August night. Even though he had already known, that was the night Larkin had told him she had leukemia.

CHAPTER 3

Letter #5 - August 2, 2011

My perfect friend,

You came to see me last night. I had poured myself a cup of coffee, grabbed that day's edition of The Philadelphia Daily News, and made my way onto the balcony of my fourth-floor hotel room, which has become my home in the past month. Most people read the newspaper in the morning, but, as you know, I always read it before I go to bed. I am certainly not a morning person, and I never have time to just sit and read in the mornings before I leave for work. Well, when I worked. I always try to capture every last little bit of sleep I can before getting out of bed. Like always, I went straight for the Sports section followed, of course, by the Entertainment section. I always try to keep up-to-date with what is going on in your corner of the world, if not just to see who you might be dating this week. I know, I know. I can be hard on you.

As I sat on the balcony, I took notice of the beautiful view that was laid out before me. My balcony is just high enough to reach above the treetops, giving me a picturesque view of the Delaware River. Last night was especially breathtaking. It was as if I was looking at a painting. The cloudless sky gave way to the full moon, and the stars blanketed the normally muddy brown-colored river, turning it into a radiant white glow. I could see the lights emanating off the Camden skyline just across the river. I would glance up from the newspaper every so often, allowing the view to infuse into my memory. There was nothing more perfect, more beautiful, than this masterpiece laid out before me.

Suddenly, a knock at the door had startled me, and I figured it was Chris or maybe my mother. Never in a million years did I expect to see you. I haven't seen you in so long, and just one glimpse of your perfect face made my heart skip a beat. It was at that moment that I realized I had been proven wrong. There actually was something more perfect, more beautiful than the masterpiece I had just left behind on that balcony moments ago.

When you looked at me, I felt as if you were reading my mind. I was so happy to see you, and I couldn't wait to wrap my arms around you. I remember, as I tried to release myself from our embrace, I felt you squeeze me tighter. I, of course, reciprocated, trying to dissolve the seven months' time in which I hadn't been able to disappear into your arms. You didn't say anything, and this worried me. You just held onto me for a long while. I felt your head bury into my shoulder, and I suddenly realized you were crying. I have never seen you cry before, Ryan.

I asked you to tell me what was wrong, and you begged me to talk to you. Talk to you? I didn't know what to think about first, but then I realized you knew. Damn it, you knew. I then realized it had to have been your mom who told you. How else would you know?

I am so sorry I didn't tell you, Ryan. The sorrow in your eyes broke my heart. I should have told you. You should have heard it from me. I beg your forgiveness. I was scared. I didn't want to be a burden to you. I could tell you were angry with me. Two months was too long to wait.

I watched you as you stood up and walked outside to the balcony. I waited a few minutes to see if you would come back inside. When I realized you weren't, I reluctantly walked outside and sat down next to you. Neither of us said anything for the longest time. In the distance, I could see the red lights glowing from the boats that were taking an evening cruise on the river. It made me think of the boat rides we would take together back in Somers Point.

I tried to change the subject by talking about memories of us fishing, but you know me so well, Ryan. You brushed my conversation aside. You didn't want to talk about fishing. Of course, you didn't. I could tell you were still angry. I could feel the coldness coming from your beautiful brown eyes, unlike the usual warmth I feel when you look at me.

I am so sorry, Ryan. I was going to tell you. I was just trying to find the right time. Please don't be mad at me. I really needed my best friend last night, and you were there. You saw me cry. You knew how sorry I was. I felt you put your arm around my waist, and I gently let my head fall onto your shoulder. You said to me, "Lark, I'm not mad. How can I be mad?" And you wiped a tear away from my cheek.

As I began to cry harder, you picked me up and carried me back inside to the recliner. You sat down and held me in your lap as I buried my head into your chest. You didn't say a word. You just let me cry for as long as I needed as we rocked back and forth in the recliner. I'll never forget the next thing you whispered to me. You promised me you will be here for me whenever I need you, and that you are never going to leave me alone....

The memory of that night diverted his attention away from the letter. That night was one of the worst moments of Ryan's life. He remembered it as clear as day. How could he not? He placed the letter down on his lap. He remembered. He remembered holding her as they sat on the recliner, and he had started to doze off when he had felt Larkin stir. He was still holding her while she had fallen asleep, but she had gotten cold and was shivering, so he carried her to her bed so she could get warm. *God, the memory was so vivid.* It was as if he could still feel her shivering in his arms. He had noticed she fell asleep again as he carried her to her bedroom. He gently laid her down on her bed and took her sandals and her sweatshirt off. As he tucked her in, he knelt down beside her and kissed her forehead. He stared at her for a long time while stroking her hair. She had looked so peaceful. He couldn't believe what was happening. It was unimaginable. He hadn't wanted to wake her, so he quietly made his way to her bedroom door. As he began to slowly close the door, he had heard her call for him.

"Ryan?"

He pushed the door open. "Yeah?"

"Will you stay with me? Please?"

He didn't even need to think twice about it. "Of course I will." He slipped his shoes off and climbed in next to her. She rolled over to face him, and he wrapped her up in his arms. She felt so small, smaller than he had remembered. He had felt her heart pounding, and he had hoped the day would never come when he could no longer feel her heartbeat.

Ryan continued to finish the letter.

I woke up in your arms this morning. You held me all night. You are so good to me. I have to admit I feel relieved that you now know. A weight has been lifted off my shoulders, and having you in my life, in my corner, I feel like I can do anything.

We had a bad day today, Ryan. It started out pretty great actually. You got out of the shower, and you brought me coffee as I sat out on the balcony. It was a cloudy morning and not as oppressive as yesterday. I could feel your eyes studying me during the pauses in our many different conversations. I knew you knew I had been crying while you were in the shower. I never try to cry in front of you, but I can feel myself weakening and weakening by the minute. I am definitely not as strong as I used to be. You reached over the small round table that sat between our patio chairs and grabbed my hand, and you said nothing. Ryan, you always say it best when you say nothing at all. Just the way you held my hand was enough to let me know you were ready to listen whenever I was ready to talk.

I am so angry, Ryan. You left. You just got up and left. I know I pushed you away. It's my fault, I know, but if you only knew how much I need you. You pressed and pressed me to talk to you about what I was thinking. You pressed me to tell you about my plan. I tried to explain to you that I couldn't follow the plan. You didn't want to hear it when I told you I couldn't do the chemotherapy because of not having any insurance and just like I knew you would, you offered to pay for it. I tried to tell you that I can't accept your money, Ryan. I am not a charity case. I will not take advantage of you. This is not your problem.

But you still pressed and pressed me. You begged me to let you help. You told me it was your problem too, whether I liked it or not. I could tell I had hurt you when I accused you of thinking of me as a charity case. You asked me what I would do if the situation was reversed, and you're right, Ryan. You are so right. I would do anything for you, but I just can't seem to take your money. You pleaded with me. You told me you had more money than you knew what to do with, and now you know. You want to help me, but I can't. I can't take it. I know you don't care about it, but I will never be able to pay you back. I know you're angry with me for pushing you away.

The last words you said to me today before you left are haunting me. I can't even sleep. I told you that taking your money wasn't an option for me, and you told me that letting me die wasn't an option for you. That's the last thing you said before you left. You couldn't even look at me as you grabbed your bag and packed up your things. You let the door close behind you without as much as a glance back at me. Where did you go, Ryan?

Ryan placed the book, Larkin's manuscript, and his watch back into the nightstand and slammed the drawer shut. He had a hard time catching his breath. Maybe he wasn't ready. Or maybe he just didn't want to be ready. Why couldn't she be here to read to him? She always read to him when he was in a bad place. He wanted so badly to hear her voice. He was having a hard time admitting that was not going to happen. He didn't know what to do. He was so lost, and he had no idea how to get to where he needed to go, wherever *that* was. Larkin would know. She would know what to do to help him. She was the light he needed to guide him to the place where he could find peace again. These thoughts were attacking his mind. It was as if bombs were igniting in his brain, and he was trying to find shelter, but he couldn't run fast enough. The shelter he was seeking was Larkin, but she wasn't there.

"Not yet, Larkin. I'm not ready yet," he quietly said to himself as the tears began to form behind his eyes. "Don't rush me."

He sat on the edge of the bed looking around the room. He wasn't quite sure what it was he was looking for, but he was grasping for anything that would help him get through this moment. The memories of that night in the last letter were exploding in his mind. He remembered staring into her eyes hoping she would see the desperation in his, but she had broken that stare by looking down and wouldn't look at him after that. He was so angry with her. How could she be so selfish? He knew there was nothing more he could say to her. He had reluctantly let go of her hands, grabbed his bag, and left without a word. He had never felt so helpless, even betrayed. He felt by her not letting him help her, she was betraying their friendship. He crouched down to the hallway floor just outside her door to catch his breath, and then he eventually made his way down to the hotel lobby. He had felt so disoriented. He didn't know where to go from there. He went outside and went for a walk, and he had no idea where he was going, but he didn't care at that point. He just needed to clear his head. He was losing his best friend, and he had felt so alone.

He remembered walking about a half mile before he found his way to a park bench just overlooking the Delaware River. As he rested and tried to gather his thoughts, his attention would wander from the boats and Jet Skiers buzzing by down the river to young kids playing catch with their fathers, to mothers pushing their toddlers on a nearby swing set, to several couples laughing and smiling as they walked hand-in-hand down the gravel pathway outlining the riverbanks. As he watched life happen around him, he realized this was what life was supposed to be all about. It was about being with people you love and doing everything you can to make them happy. But he had been away. Far away from the people that he had loved. He wanted Larkin to experience all these things that were happening around him. But how could she do that all alone? He had felt guilty about leaving her there without saying a word. He had done the exact opposite of what he told her he was going to do. He had told her he would never leave her alone, and that's exactly what he did.

Ryan walked back to the hotel to see Larkin again. He was going to make one last effort to help her, but if she still refused, he would do whatever it was she wanted him to do. He had knocked on her door several times, but she never came to open it. He had made several attempts before he realized she was not coming. He deserved it, he thought. He had left her alone. She had every reason to not come to that door. He felt his heart drop into his stomach, and he had never felt more alone than right at that moment. Walking away from that hotel room door was one of the hardest things he had ever done.

He had gotten himself a room to stay in before he headed back to South Africa the next morning. He was exhausted from all the traveling the past two days, but his mind and heart were so full of anguish, he couldn't help but toss and turn. He couldn't sleep, and the only person who could help him was Larkin. He had needed her, more than she could ever know. Maybe if she knew, maybe if she understood how much he needed her then she would reconsider. She was always there for him, so why would this time be any different? He looked at the time. It was 12:15 a.m. He didn't care that it was late. He quickly got dressed and walked to her room. He banged on the door so loudly, he could hear people yelling at him to knock it off from inside their rooms across the hall. But he didn't care.

"*Larkin!*" he shouted. "Open the door." He kept banging the door. "Larkin, I am not leaving until you open the door!" He kept banging until he saw the light turn on underneath the doorway, giving him an immediate sense of relief.

The door opened.

"Ryan, what are you doing here? It's late." Her eyes had a blackness to them.

He pushed the door open and stormed inside. "I don't care how late it is, Larkin." He paced back and forth trying to figure out exactly what he was going to say.

"Now, I have one last thing to say to you,

and you're going to listen. No more interrupting me by telling me 'no, Ryan.' Just listen to what I have to say, okay?" He could tell she was tired and bothered, but she still gave him a nod, letting him know she was okay with it.

"I couldn't sleep tonight. This was the first night in a while that I couldn't sleep, and the only thing I could think of was you and how much I needed you. I wanted and needed you to read to me. And then I realized, what am I going to do if you're not here, Larkin? Who am I going to call when I land the role of a lifetime? Who's going to walk the red carpet with me at my premieres? Who am I going to go to when I need to get away from it all? Who's going to laugh at my jokes even when you know how stupid they are? Who's going to read to me when I can't sleep? But most importantly, Larkin, who's going to be my best friend? Don't you see? I need you, Larkin. I need you to live," he paused, catching his breath and fighting back tears. "I need you to at least *try* to live. Please, blue eyes, please let me help you." He waited for her to respond. She was also fighting back tears, but she didn't say anything. She just looked at him.

"Please, if not for you, then for me."

She looked down as she started to cry. He reached out and lifted her chin up so he could make eye contact with her again. "It's okay, Larkin. It's going to be okay."

"Okay," she finally whispered reluctantly as the tears ran down her face.

"Okay?" he asked to make sure he heard her correctly.

She nodded yes. "Okay. For you."

He wiped her tears and pulled her into his arms. He knew that was probably the hardest thing she had ever done.

Letter #6 - August 3, 2011

Dear Ryan,

You came back to see me early this morning. I know you thought you woke me, but you didn't. I couldn't sleep. You have since left to head back to South Africa. God, why do you have to be so far away? I just want to thank you, Ryan. Thank you for being you. Thank you for being the most generous human being. I am just happy to know you. Happy to know that people like you exist. You offered to pay for my chemotherapy again, and, although I swore I would not accept your help, the words that came out of your mouth were impossible to say no to. I don't want to die, Ryan. I know you think I was giving up by not accepting your help, but that wasn't the case. Being sick is bad. Being sick and not having health insurance is worse. But disappointing you? Leaving you behind without a fight? Being alone? Leaving you alone? That's improbable. I promise I will do my best to live. If not for me, then for you. As I fight the biggest battle life has to offer, I promise I will tell you everything. I will write you everything, but you must promise me some things, Ryan. If I am not so lucky as to beat this, if I don't live, promise me you'll live on for me. Promise me you will live the most incredible life, meet the most incredible people, see the most incredible places, and make the most incredible movies. And lastly, promise me you will stop all this nonsensical dating you do and fall so in love with someone that you can't imagine living without her. Life is incomplete without love. Find it, catch it, hold onto it, nurture it, and never let it go.

CHAPTER 4

Letter #7 - August 22, 2011

Hey, Fish,

Just a short letter. I spoke with you today. Your voice has a healing tone. Just hearing it makes me smile. You told me today you were able to get some time off so you can come to my first chemo treatment with me. I didn't say it to you, but I am so relieved. I need you there. I need you to hold my hand. I don't want you to know how scared I really am. You always tell me how strong I am, but I don't feel strong. You are my strength, and I can't wait to see you, although it's a shame I am going to see you under these circumstances. Three more weeks.

Letter #8 - September 11, 2011

Hey, Ry Guy,

Tomorrow is the big day. Treatment one of six. I am so glad you are going to be there. It means so much to me you are traveling all this way just to be here. You are traveling almost an entire day just to spend a few hours with me.

Have I told you how amazing you are? Why are you so good to me?

I am scared, Ryan. Terrified. I sort of have an idea of what to expect. Being a nurse helps, and I have been reading the brochures that the doctors gave me. But no matter how many preparations I have had, my fear is insurmountable.

I spoke with Chris today. He found out the news. He expressed his concern and sorrows. He said that if he had only known sooner, he would have done things differently. That's exactly what I didn't want. I don't want someone there because they feel obligated. I want someone there because they want to be. And you want to be. You have always been there. Thank you for always being there.

I will see you tomorrow, and I will do my best to be strong.

Letter #9 - September 12, 2011

Ryan,

Well, it's here. The second Monday of the month. The first day of the hardest journey of my life is about to begin. The scream from the alarm clock was loud enough to wake the entire hotel. My head shot straight up off of my pillow, and for a moment, I didn't know where I was. It was pitch-

black, and the lights that did shine in the darkness were a blinding blur. I looked over and squinted at the alarm clock as I shut it off.

Just 6:00 a.m. I barely got any sleep, tossing and turning with every subtle noise that emerged from the hallway, from the thin hotel walls, from the drift of the curtains blowing from the breeze coming through the window. As I rolled back over, I gathered my thoughts and tried to make sense of the day I was about to journey through. I had no expectations, and I figured I was better off hoping for the best but expecting the worst.

I drew myself a warm bath, and as the mountains of bubbles swallowed my body, the wonder of whether or not you would change your mind consumed my thoughts. I know how busy you are, and you certainly have no obligation to me. It has been six weeks since that night you came to see me, and although we speak almost every other day, we don't speak much about my sickness. You promised me you would be here with me at my first treatment, and although I truly want you to be there, I always make sure you don't feel like you have to. But you keep assuring me over and over again that you will be here.

As I towel-dried off after my bath, I heard a knock at the door. I quickly slipped into my robe, approached the door, and although I would have given anything to see you standing on the other side, I felt an overwhelming sense of comfort and safety as I stared at the beautiful woman standing before me—my mother Joan.

I look up to my mother more than any other person, and I aspire to be just like her. As you know, she is very protective of me, her baby daughter—even though I didn't quite turn out like she had hoped. If it were up to her, I would have been captain of the cheerleading team and homecoming and prom queen just as she was when she was in high school. But I know she loves me just the same and has supported every decision I have ever made. After all, it is my mother's maiden name that I am named after.

As my mother waited for me to get ready to leave for the hospital, I struggled to find what to wear. I wanted to dress comfortably because I didn't quite know how long I would be in the hospital and what exactly was going to happen. As I dug through the dresser drawers, I noticed your black and gray OCNJ sweatshirt you had given me a long time ago. Perfect. If you don't show up, if you do change your mind, then at least I would still feel close to you. I also slipped into a pair of cream-colored sweatpants, and I stepped into my gray and pink flip-flops. You know, the ones you laughed at when I bought them.

I've had an uneasiness in my stomach all morning as I think about the chemotherapy. The nervousness severs through my appetite like a machete even though I know it is in my best interest to eat something. But the thought of food just ties the rope in my stomach tighter. I am glad my mother is with me, but I really need you to be here.

I am writing to you as I sit in the passenger seat of my mom's Land Rover. The freeway is jam-packed, and we are stop-and-go as we navigate our way to the hospital in the midst of rush-hour traffic. Let me take you along as Joan and I have a conversation. This will be fun, don't you think? Remember, I said I was going to tell you everything.

"Is Ryan coming, honey?" my mother pries as she concentrates on the traffic-filled Philadelphia freeway.

"He said he would be there. I hope he comes," I said.

"Well, can you blame him if he doesn't? He certainly shouldn't have to deal with this. At least he wants to help you financially. That was very generous of him and absolutely unnecessary. I'm surprised you asked."

"I didn't ask," I immediately responded with resentment in my voice. "He offered, and I reluctantly accepted."

"He offered? Really?" My mother always liked you, Ryan, but for some reason, she always seemed to make me feel like I wasn't good enough for you. Maybe if I had become that cheerleader, that homecoming and prom queen, then my mother would feel differently.

"Besides, Larkin, he is in South Africa. That is a lot to expect from him to travel all this way. And anyway, he needs to focus on keeping himself out of the tabloids with all these women that he dates."

I didn't feel the need to respond to her snarky comment. I instead stared out the window and prayed you would come. I started to think maybe my mother was right. Maybe you shouldn't have to deal with this. You have your own life to live. You never really talk to me about the women that you date, but I am well aware. It's hard not to be when your pictures are always in the magazines with different models and actresses. I never know who is coming and going. But how can I blame you? You're allowed to date. I know you are still reeling from your divorce, and I imagine you're lonely. I know I am. But, Ryan, I do hope you will eventually settle down soon.

I felt my mother place her hand on my knee. "Well, maybe he will come. I hope he does. I know you really want him to." She must have seen the sadness in my face after her last comment. I know she doesn't fully understand the friendship that you and I share, so I am quick to let go of the resentment I am feeling at this moment. We just pulled into the parking lot of the hospital, and I can barely breathe. I'll continue my letter when I get inside and settled...

...As we made our way across the car-filled parking lot, I intertwined my arm with Joan's. I felt like everything was moving in slow motion, and it seemed like it took ages to get to the entrance of the building. My mother must have felt me trembling because she unlocked my grasp on her arm and instead wrapped her arm around my waist and held me close to her as we entered into the elevator.

The air in the hospital was frigid, and I was glad I had the sweatshirt you had given me. My mother and I checked in, and the nurse, Rose, guided us to a room where I was to get my blood drawn. Rose was very nice. She is middle-aged. I would guess maybe forty-five. But she has a comforting smile and a soft voice that can put anybody at ease. I hope she is my nurse every time I come. The white-walled hallways were uninviting and cold, and the white-tiled floors underneath my feet felt hard as cement. Rose took us into a laboratory room where she drew my blood to see if I am even healthy enough to get chemo today. After she finished, my mom and I went to the snack room to get something to eat, and then we walked the grounds as we waited to find out if I would indeed be getting treatment. About forty-five minutes passed before I was startled by the beep sounding from the pager, alerting us to come back inside. The last thing I wanted to do was to leave the beautiful and colorful landscape of the hospital grounds and go back into the colorless, unwelcoming hallways. We entered into what they called the infusion room to get ready for my treatment. This room was a little more friendly and inviting with a flat- screen TV, windows, and a huge brown recliner that could probably sit three of me.

As I got comfortable, Rose began to set me up with the IV. I couldn't help but feel sad and disappointed that you hadn't come. I figured you would have been here by now or at least left me a message that you were running late. But maybe you're not able to. After all, you are coming from

South Africa, and I knew it was hard for you to get time off from filming. But then again you would have called if you weren't able to come, wouldn't you? Well, maybe you just didn't want to after all. Maybe it is too much for you to deal with, and you changed your mind, and you didn't want to hurt me.

I must have let my mind drift away into slumber as my mother held my hand while she read a book because the last thing I remember is awakening to the squeeze of her hand. As I turned my head to look over at her, I saw you standing above me, and at that moment, I thought for certain I had to be dreaming. But if this really was my dream, I certainly wouldn't be here, that's for sure. I remember I clenched my eyes shut for a couple of seconds to work the blurriness out, and as my vision cleared, I saw you mouth the word "hi" to me as you tucked a loose strand of hair behind my ear. As always, the perfection of your face made my heart skip a beat, and I couldn't help but smile at you. "Hi," I whispered back. Your face was tired, but still, nothing less than perfect.

You touched my shoulder and guided me toward the other side of the recliner for three, and you climbed in next to me and wrapped your arm around my shoulders. "Sorry, I'm late," you said.

I buried the back of my head into your solid, muscular chest, and you rested your chin on the top of my head. I love that you are so much taller than me. My head always seems to fit perfectly underneath your chin every time we hug, and this time was no different. You came, Ryan. I can't believe you came. Why are you so good to me?

"Of course I came. I said I would," you said to me.

"How did you get the time off?"

"Don't worry about it, Larkin. Right now at this point in my life, you come first, and I will sacrifice anything to get to you when you need me, okay?" I could feel the vibration of your vocal chords through the back of my head as you spoke to me. You turned your face toward me and gently kissed me on the side of my head. I looked over at my mother, and as our eyes met, she gave me a smile and a nod, and at that moment, I knew she now understood the bond that you and I shared.

CHAPTER 5

Letter #10 - September 15, 2011

Dear Ryan,

One down, five to go. That's what I kept telling myself two days ago as I struggled to pick my legs up into the bed. Ryan, I was so sick, so exhausted. My fragile body didn't want to work right. So this is what it's like. I had always read about cancer and chemotherapy in my nursing books and in the pamphlets the doctors had given me, but they certainly didn't give the disease nor its potential killer any justice. I decided at that exact moment—the fifth time I had gotten sick that day—that this opponent had garnered my full attention, my full respect. Growing up an athlete, I had always been a fierce competitor mainly due to my father always preaching to me about fearlessness and never backing down no matter how big the challenge was. But this challenge, this is bigger than not giving up the winning drive to the basket in the basketball championship, or not striking out when your team is down one run with two outs and the bases loaded in the bottom of the seventh. This is life or death. And I certainly want to live. It had only been twenty-four hours since the chemo treatment, and the last twelve hours had been as dreadful of a time as I had ever experienced. I can't imagine that it can get any worse. I finally decided that lying on my back was a comfortable position, for the time being anyway. I looked around the room that had been my haven as a kid growing up. After I moved out, my parents turned it into a guest room, so there is nothing familiar about it anymore. Everything is new—a new bed, new furniture, even the hardwood floors are new. But it does give off a sense of homeliness with its cottage-type decor—a white dresser and two nightstands with chipped paint, giving them a rustic glow, a decorative brown aluminum star hanging on the wall just over the head of the bed, and a big open window giving way to the bright sunshine. But it's the finishing touches of the multi-colored calla lilies that my father must have placed throughout the room when my mother and I were at the hospital that are my favorite. As you know, Ryan, my father is a hard man, but when it comes to me, he has a soft spot. He is the compassionate one while Joan has always been the disciplinarian. He had always wanted a son, and although he raised me as a tomboy, he always treats me like a lady.

I am so happy my parents have always had a happy marriage. I have always admired the way my father treats my mother, and no matter how long they have been married, they always act as if they are newlyweds. My father, always brought my mother a fresh bouquet of flowers home every week, and he still does to this day. Every time I would come home to visit, I would take notice of the fresh arrangement sitting as the centerpiece on the dining room table. Roses, lilies, sunflowers, daisies, carnations. Every week it was different, and it depended on the season too. My father has always been attentive toward my mother's needs and desires, and he does everything he can to make her happy. In turn, my mother reciprocates his kindness, and she does everything she can to make sure he is happy, too. My father is such a hard worker, and he always made sure there was food on the table and clothes on our backs. Being the battalion chief of the Atlantic City Fire Department meant working long days and being on call twenty-four hours a day, seven days a week. When he was called away, he always promised me he would make it home that night, and he never once broke that promise. I have always thought of my father as invincible, and I never really found myself being too scared for his life when he was working. He is the epitome of everything I want in a man, and I had always hoped the man I would marry would be just like him.

As I laid on the bed, I could feel the sickness coming on again, and the spinning blades of the ceiling fan above me were not helping. I quickly rolled to the side of the bed and lowered myself to the floor. Crawling to the bathroom, I couldn't help but think of how grateful I was to my parents for deciding to add on a bathroom to the bedroom when they redesigned it. They did leave me a bucket next to the bed, but I wanted to avoid having to use that if at all possible. I cringed at the thought of either one of them having to clean that out. After the toxins exited my body, I knew I did not have the energy to crawl back to the bed, and besides, my knees were too sore and bruised from the crawling back and forth on the hardwood floor all day. I just wanted to get some sleep to make this feeling go away, and at that point, I didn't care where, so I decided the bathroom floor was as good a place as any. As I curled up into a ball on the cold, gray, tile floor, I could only think of one thing that could possibly make me feel any better—and you were half a world away. I can't quite understand the feeling I was having for you. I longed for you to be there. I longed to see your perfect face. I yearned for you to nurture me and to protect me. It was a feeling much different than I had ever felt for Chris. It was deeper, it was intense, and it was mysterious. As I lay on the cold bathroom floor, I struggled, wanting to keep my eyes open and to stay awake so that the sleep wouldn't cut off my thoughts of you. My thoughts of you were what kept me going. But as I succumbed to the battle that I was having with keeping my eyes open, I gave in and slowly let them close, and as they did, I prayed to God that maybe I would see you in my dreams.

This last letter struck Ryan like a lightning bolt upon the earth. To imagine her suffering like that killed him. Neither of them had known what to expect, and the doctor had told them that everyone responded differently to the chemotherapy. He had wanted to be there those days following her first chemo treatment, but he wasn't able to stay with her. He had to fly back to South Africa to get back to work. Even though he had been half a world away from her, she was never far from his heart.

It had been sixteen hours since the plane took off out of Philadelphia and touched down half a world away in Cape Town, South Africa, but with the time difference, it was more like twenty-two hours. Ryan had been able to stay with Larkin for only a couple of hours after her chemo treatment before he had to head back to work. To most people, the time and the energy to travel twenty-four hours one way to spend only a few hours is not worth it, but Ryan wasn't most people. Besides, he had promised Larkin he would be there, and he had known what he was getting himself into. He had tried to get more time off, but the director, Leon Lewis, was demanding, and the film was on a deadline. He was thrilled when he was told he could have *two* days. He knew he could make it work where he could at least spend some time with her.

He remembers it was a tough good-bye when Larkin and Joan had dropped him off at the airport. It had haunted him on the plane ride home. He had sensed that Larkin hadn't wanted to let go when he hugged her good-bye. He knew she didn't know what to expect in the coming days and neither did he, and he had wanted to be there to help her. She had understood, of course. She always did. He didn't want to leave her. It was the first time he had difficulty letting her go. He had looked into her blue eyes and saw an ocean of strength and courage that amazed him. He was proud of her and the way she was handling things. He was proud at how she hadn't flinched one millimeter when they pulled the IV out of her arm, or how she hadn't seemed to be too scared when they told her she was more than likely to get pretty sick that night.

He remembers the conversation on the phone that night that had uncovered an awareness that had been buried inside his heart since he was a child. He looked at his watch as he entered into his hotel room and set his single luggage bag down next to the couch. His time was 3:00 p.m., 9:00 a.m. her time. Maybe, just maybe, she'd be awake to answer his call, he had thought. He walked out onto his balcony overlooking the waterfront and took in a breath of fresh air. Although he had missed his home, he was mesmerized by all the beauty that surrounded him. The hotel he had stayed in was perfectly positioned along a private waterside platform alongside the edge of a port that extended into the Table Bay. That particular afternoon, the sun was just in the right position to draw out the illuminating orange that colored the mountainside that sat just to his left, and the sun's rays extended out to the marina that was directly in front of him. The glare of the sun off one of the yacht's windows in the marina had caught his attention. It was then that his attention had immediately shifted to Larkin and all they had shared in their past. They were raised in a haze of sun and sand and boats and fishing, and Larkin had always told Ryan about her dreams of owning her own yacht one day. He worried that maybe that dream would never happen for her.

As he made the phone call, the disappointment that had set in by the time the fourth ring had ended was quickly replaced with relief when he heard a familiar voice on the other line answer hello. Although it wasn't the voice he had been wanting, nor expecting, to hear. After all, it was *her* cell phone. It was still nice to know someone was there with her.

"Hey, Mr. Wilson. It's Ryan."

"I know, Ryan. How are you? You made it back safely, I assume?" Ryan knew Russell had always liked him mainly because he always looked out for his daughter when they were kids.

"Yes, sir, I did. Thank you. I was hoping to speak with Larkin. Is she awake?"

"I'm sorry, Ryan, she isn't. She's pretty sick. She's been up all night, and I really don't want to wake her now that she is finally asleep."

"Okay." The disappointment that had left him moments ago had conveniently made its way back into his gut. *Up all night? Pretty sick?* That was definitely not what he had wanted to hear. "I see. Well, can you please tell her I called and was asking for her?"

"Absolutely, Ryan. I will."

As he started to pull the phone away from his ear, he could hear Russell start to say something.

"Ryan, I wanted to thank you personally for what you have done for my daughter. Not for just helping her financially, but for being there with her yesterday. I know my daughter, and I know she didn't ask you for help, which means you did this all on your own. You are a good man, Ryan."

Those words had stirred up an array of emotions inside Ryan's soul. He certainly had not felt like a good man. Larkin was at home fighting for her life, and he was out living the life. Traveling the world. Making movies. Making millions of dollars. Dating a different supermodel every month since his divorce. He didn't have a worry in the world. He struggled to respond to the kind words that Mr. Wilson had just extended to him.

"Thank you, sir. That means a lot. Really." He immediately hung up the phone, not wanting Russell to hear the cracking in his voice.

After he had hung up the phone with Russell, Ryan made his way through the French doors that opened up into the spacious private dining area of his one-bedroom suite. Just to his left was a separate lounge area which housed a fifty-inch flat-screen TV, a fully-stocked minibar, and a mini-library with his own personal selection of books. The lounge connected the dining room to the bedroom, which had another set of French doors leading out onto another private balcony. Elegant marble bathrooms with antique toiletries and fresh flowers throughout the suite highlighted the luxury Ryan had come to know as part of his everyday lifestyle.

He grabbed his luggage bag and carried it into the bedroom. He had noticed the voicemail light flickering on the hotel phone on the nightstand next to his king-sized bed. He was careful to not give out his cell phone number to just anybody, so if anybody other than family or friends or his agent and publicist needed to reach him, they called the main hotel number. And if they didn't know the hotel number, they called his publicist. Three messages—one from the front desk welcoming him back from his two-day trip and asking if he needed anything, and two from Ada, a South African model he had met on the set just one week prior. She had wanted to know if he was free that evening. He had deleted all three messages, not taking the time to write down Ada's number. She was young—ten years his junior—but she seemed nice, and there was no question about how beautiful she was. But the words that Mr. Wilson had just said to him about being a good man kept circling around his mind.

He couldn't help but think of Larkin and her lying in bed sick and exhausted, probably crying and tossing and turning. He hadn't wanted to go out with Ada that night; he had wanted to go out with Larkin. He had wanted to show Larkin everything he had been able to see the last ten years of his life. He had wanted to walk her around downtown Cape Town and introduce her to new cuisines and new cultures. He had wanted to bring her to the set and introduce her to his world. He had shared bits and pieces of his world with her throughout his career. She had been to many of his movie premieres, and she had become close to his three best friends—Ian, Sarah, and Justin—but that was only a taste. He had wanted her to experience all of it. They had shared an amazing childhood together. They had been in their own little world, and now they were worlds apart. Unfortunately, it had taken a tragedy to open his eyes. It had taken a tragedy to make him realize that he not only had wanted to show her his world, but in fact, he had wanted to be her world.

CHAPTER 6

The wind gust was so hard it thrust open the French doors inside the bedroom, wrenching Ryan out of his sleep. He didn't even remember falling asleep, but he was thrilled he was able to get some rest. He had spent most of the night reading Larkin's letters. The more and more he read them, the more and more intoxicating they became. They had brought back many memories, and he hadn't wanted to put them down. It was as if she was sitting there right next to him talking to him. He looked over at the clock. It was 6:30 a.m.

Ryan immediately picked up right where he left off. He felt a sense of urgency to finish reading these letters. He was searching for closure, and for some reason, he was sure these letters would get him there. He had been yearning for her. To see her face. To feel her touch. He wanted her to come back and haunt him. These letters were her ghost.

Letter #11 - October 16, 2011

Hey, Buddy,

It's the second Sunday of October, and I am watching you sleep. Today was a perfect day. I am so glad we were able to spend the day together. It was only this morning when I was anxiously awaiting for your plane to land at the Atlantic City International Airport. I don't have to be in Philadelphia until 11:00 a.m. tomorrow morning, so you and I are able to stay at my parents' house tonight before heading out in the morning. Unfortunately, my parents are out of town for the next three days helping my sister, Laura, move from Baltimore to New York City for a new job, so you won't be able to visit with them. I know my father really would like to see you. But the one good thing from it is that you are spending the next three days with me until they get back. I haven't seen you since my first chemo treatment one month ago, and I could feel the butterflies fluttering around in my stomach as I waited for you at the baggage claim. I have been feeling okay the past couple of weeks but not before I battled through three days of sickness that I wouldn't wish upon my worst enemy. I've noticed that I have a harder time getting over a cold, and I have also noticed that just the slightest bump on my arm or leg leaves a collage of purples and yellows on my skin for days.

As I waited patiently in the crowded baggage claim area, I couldn't help but feel guilty and confused about the thoughts that were going through my head. I felt like this disease was punishment for something that I may have done in my past. But I don't really know what. Maybe for my marriage failing. Maybe for not following my dream of being a writer. Maybe for...oh, I don't know. But what I do know or feel was that this disease could be a blessing in disguise. If it weren't for the cancer, I wouldn't be seeing you as much as I am now. I know, I know, Ryan. It's a pretty morbid thought. But I can't deny it. I obviously don't want to have cancer, but I do know that on the second Sunday of every month for the next four months, I am going to see you. And I couldn't be happier.

You want to know something? Just as I saw you turn the corner just at the bottom of the escalator earlier today, I couldn't take my eyes off of you. Your high cheekbones give way to your narrow jawline and your brown eyes complement your infamous crooked smile. You were dressed as fashionably as ever, but then again, you always are, aren't you? You had black jeans on with a cool blue plaid shirt, slightly unbuttoned at the top, revealing a white tank underneath, and your sleeves were rolled up to your elbows. Your perfect face was complemented with a gray newsboy cap, and your casual black Converse Chucks lightened up your look. As your eyes finally met mine, you gave me that crooked smile with your lips pressed together, as well as a quick wink of your left eye that sat underneath your furrowed brow. It was at that exact moment, the moment when I couldn't look away from you, that I realized maybe this was the reason for my punishment. That I had loved you and I had always loved you even though I had been married to another.

"Hi," you mouthed to me as you dropped your carry-on bag on the floor next to you, quickly lifting me up as you embraced me. "You look good, Larkin," you said, and I could hear relief in your voice. I think you were expecting me to look sickly.

I couldn't help but smile at you as I said hello back. We stared at each other for a moment before walking outside to my car, and you took my portfolio bag off my shoulder and draped it across yours, alongside your carry-on bag. I never carry a purse. Sometimes a backpack or a portfolio bag but never a purse. You always liked that I am more of a grab-my-cash-or-cards-and-put-them-in-my-back-pocket-and-go kind of girl. As we walked side-by-side, I could feel your hand occasionally brush mine, and it sent a shock of excitement all the way up my arm into my chest. All I wanted to do was just take your hand into mine and interlace our fingers together, but wanting and doing are two totally different things. Despite what you think, I have never been brave, especially when it comes to you. I actually had wondered if maybe you were purposely brushing my hand because you had wanted to grab my hand too, but when I glanced over at you and down to your hand, I had noticed you hid it in your pocket. It was as if you were reading my mind and saying back to me, "Forget it, I don't want to hold your hand." Of course not, why would you? I asked myself. As we approached the car, I asked you to drive, and you, of course, accepted. I handed you my set of keys—five keys to be exact. One to open and start the car, one to my parents' house, one to the house I used to share with Chris (I really should give that one back, huh?), one to my locker at the gym that unfortunately I haven't been able to go to much lately, and the fifth and final key is to your house in Los Angeles. "Just in case you ever decided to come visit," you had said to me about three years ago when you bought the house with Abigail. But I, of course, never stayed with you when I did come to visit, mainly out of respect for Chris.

We only had about a twenty-minute drive to my parents' house, but I still pulled my manuscript out of my portfolio bag anyway. I could sense you peeking over, trying to see what it was I was doing. I looked over at you, showed you the manuscript, and you acknowledged me with that crooked smile. God, I love your smile. And you gave me a nod, letting me know that you wanted me to read it to you.

"It's been a while," I offered.

"Too long," you agreed.

It had been too long, almost eight months, since I last read to you. I picked up where I left off—when Jillian led Nathan into the room that would change everything. I proceeded to finish the chapter and start the next one, and neither of us budged when you parked along the curb in front of my parent's two-story cape cod on Colgate Street. We sat in the car as I finished, and I could tell you were listening attentively. I could see you were truly involved in the story. It was the first time I actually read to you in person, so I was never really able to see your facial expressions or see if your eyes were really interested. After I finished the last sentence, I closed the manuscript and looked over at you. Your eyes emitted a look of approval, a look of pride.

"Larkin, it's great. Really great," you said.

"Is it okay, you think? I know you're biased."

"It has nothing to do with bias. I really do think it's great. And I would tell you if I didn't. You need to finish it."

"It's almost there, but I have been working on another project, too. But I'll tell you about that some other time."

And I will tell you sometime, Ryan. Just not yet.

I watched you as you looked all around at your surroundings. At all the neighborhood houses and the boats parked in the driveways. I could tell you were in deep thought as you watched two young boys walk down the street with a fishing rod in one hand and a tackle box in the other. It may be October, but it is never too late in the season to fish. Autumn fishing is sometimes just as fun as summer fishing, and autumn has always been your favorite time to fish. I could tell you missed home. You don't come home as much anymore, especially since your father died almost four years ago. You usually just fly your mother out to LA to see you. I know it's much easier that way. I also know you haven't been to the cemetery since your father's funeral. You never really talk about your father since his death, but despite the differences that you had regarding your career choice, you two still had a pretty strong relationship, and I know you miss him. I miss him.

I never told you this, Ryan, but I am going to tell you now. I have made it a point every year on the anniversary of your father's death to bring flowers to his grave in your honor. I also sit and read to him a recent article I had found, reviewing your latest movie and your career. I also went to visit the grave back in early February after you won best actor and placed a picture of you holding your award. I am sorry I never told you I go to see your father. It was something private between him and me.

I knew you were deep in thought because I felt your hand jump when I touched it. "Are you ready?"

"Yeah," you said. "Let's go."

You grabbed your carry-on bag and my portfolio bag as we made our way into the four-bedroom home I grew up in. We entered into the family room that was decorated with floral wall art surrounding the wicker furniture that sat atop the bamboo floor. My mother has always had a knack for interior designing, don't you think? As you took my bag up to my bedroom, I went into the kitchen to make us a pot of coffee. And as I waited for you to come down, I heard the creaking of the front screen door, and I knew you had gone outside to the front porch. I joined you several minutes later, and we sat quietly giving each other a quick glance and smile every so often as we sipped on our coffee. These had been my favorite times growing up with you. Sitting on our porches quietly, not needing to say anything to each other. Like I wrote before, Ryan, you always say it best when you say nothing at all. It's your eyes and your smile that do the talking. Every time you would give me a glance and a smile, I knew you were content and at peace. I knew everything that was going on around you since you landed was giving you a sense of nostalgia—my house, the neighborhood, the smell of the saltwater blowing in from the bay with the cool autumn breeze.

It was a cool sixty degrees, and birdsong was echoing from the half-barren trees standing above front lawns that were carpeted with the mixture of yellow, red, and orange leaves. It had rained earlier in the day, and the road was smeared with the residue of the wet leaves that were stuck on the tires of the passing cars. I noticed your attention was focused on the crowds of people that were coming and going from the house next door. There has been a "for sale" sign out front for the past two months, and today, there was an open house. There had been a middle-aged couple who had lived there for the past three and a half years before they moved out two months ago to relocate to a fifty-five-and-over community. But prior to them, it had been the home that you grew up in. It had been a second home to me, and I was sad to see the changes that had been made to the property since your mother moved out after Robert died. "It's different," I heard you quietly mumble. It sure is different, Ryan. It sure is.

You asked me if I minded if you went over to take a look, and I, of course, didn't mind at all; and although you had asked me to join you, I declined, knowing that it was something you needed to do by yourself.

I don't know what happened when you went over to your old house, but the minute you came back, you approached me as I was making us dinner in the kitchen and asked me to go dancing tonight. And I want to thank you for an amazing night. Dancing with you tonight was an escape for me. An escape from the cancer, from the loneliness, from the darkness. I can't wait for our next dance.

He couldn't help but smile as he remembered that day. Ryan had approached that two-story colonial and noticed that the shutters that were once maroon were now forest green, and the garage had been turned into a screened-in porch. The swing his father had made and lassoed to the enormous maple tree in the front yard when he was five was no longer there, and the small flower garden that sat underneath the front bay window that he and his mother would plant together every spring had been replaced by a trio of perfectly square-shaped bushes. He had entered into the four-bedroom house and immediately felt a sense of pensiveness. Not so much because it had brought back fond childhood memories, but because it was different. Nothing about it was the same as when he had walked through the house four years prior after his father's funeral. The color of the walls in the kitchen had changed from a cream yellow to a dark beige, and the hardwood floor had been replaced with white marble tile outlined with black grout. French doors had replaced the single exterior door that connected the kitchen to the garage—now the screened-in porch— and the hardwood floor in the family room that he and his older brother had helped his father lay when he was in high school had been replaced with white shag carpet. He had quietly made his way through the house, weaving his way around the crowds of people. He couldn't believe how many people had come to the open house. There were at least a dozen, he had thought, and they all had to have been in their fifties. He remembers overhearing the realtor saying a couple of times to the prospective buyers, "This is the house that Ryan Boone grew up in." He had chuckled to himself, knowing that the majority of the people there probably had no idea who Ryan Boone was. Even if they had, why in the world would that persuade them to buy the house?

He had made his way up the stairwell, noticing that the walls that used to boast pictures of him and his brothers throughout their childhood years were no longer there. Instead, there was a white blank wall of nothing. He had entered into only one room—his room—the room he had grown up in. But it really wasn't his room anymore, and he had been quickly reminded of that as soon as he stepped foot into it. In fact, it wasn't even a bedroom anymore. It had been renovated into a study with two giant bookshelves against the wall to his right filled with books from the likes of Charles Dickens, George Elliot, Jane Austen, and Stephen King. There was a medium-sized cherry oak desk with a closed laptop against the wall to his left, and there was a small French-style armchair sitting directly underneath the window on the far wall. It was the window that faced Larkin's bedroom; the window he so often would open at night time before going to sleep to talk with her about the day they had. Their houses were close enough they could easily hear each other without having to yell and wake everyone else up.

As he had approached the window to look out toward hers, he had sworn he could see a reflection of them dancing together when they were teenagers. She was healthy and happy, young and beautiful, full of life and energy. The reflection had seemed so real to him. He could hear the music as if it was playing in the room he was standing in. He could feel her hand resting on the top of his left shoulder and her left hand intertwined with his right hand as she taught him the correct steps and spins. He could hear her voice: *one-two-three, one-two-three, one-two-three, spin.* As he had watched the two of them dancing in the window, he was startled by a strange voice and a strange touch on the back of his elbow. "Can I help you with anything, sir? Do you have any questions about the house?"

"Uh, no, no. No, thank you." He had quickly darted out of the bedroom, down the steps, and out of the house. He had walked back to Larkin's house and found her cooking them dinner in the kitchen. She was at the sink, her back was turned to him, but he knew she had heard him come in through the noisy front door. "Just in time for dinner," he remembers her calling out to him. And as she had turned to face him, he had grabbed her right hand and put it on his shoulder, then took her left hand and led her into a dance. He quickly spun her around, and as she looked up at him with a smile, he had asked, "Do you want to go dancing with me tonight?"

They had danced the night away at a jazz club in Atlantic City. It had been the most fun he had had in a long time. They barely sat down the entire night, and it was so good to see Larkin laughing and smiling. But he could tell she was getting tired, and he was worried about it. She had fallen asleep on the way home, and he had carried her into the house and tucked her into bed. Before he turned the light out, he had noticed her manuscript on her nightstand. He grabbed it, sat next to her on her bed, and attempted to find where it was she had left off. As he was searching, she had grabbed his hand and pulled it away from her work in progress. "No, Ryan. You can't. I have to read it to you. Remember?"

"Okay, that's fine. I'm sorry." He closed it, put it back in the folder, and bent over to give her a goodnight kiss on the forehead. She grabbed his hand as he brushed her chin with his thumb. "Lay here with me." He positioned himself on his side to face her. He had given her a quick smile and wink whenever he would catch a quick glimpse of her blue eyes as she struggled to keep them open. He had not wanted to take his eyes off of her. Every moment he had spent with her those past two months had been an awakening. An awakening into what she had meant to him. When he had been away from her, he didn't just miss her; he missed all the little things—the way she had called him Fish, the way she had said "hey" when she answered the phone, the way she had wrapped her arms around his neck when he hugged her good-bye, the way she had smiled at him when she saw him for the first time in a long while—and he never thought that the little things would have meant everything to him.

Letter #12 - October 17, 2011

Ryan,

It's late. I remember the night of my first treatment. I was so exhausted, and I couldn't keep my eyes open. But tonight, that couldn't be more further from the truth. I would give anything to keep them closed, but I can't.

I miss you. You couldn't stay with me. You were supposed to stay with me this week, but you're not here. I keep reliving our conversation from earlier today after my treatment. You and I took a walk through the park just across the parking lot. It was a pleasant day, the breeze had subsided from the day before, and the sun's rays would make occasional short visits through the small breaks in the clouds, but not enough to fully dry the grass and the park benches from the earlier rainstorm. I wanted to rest so you took your sweatshirt off and placed it on the bench so we had a dry place to sit. I knew you had something on your mind. I could tell. You had a hard time looking me in the eyes.

Ryan, you're gone. You left. You had to, I know. I also know you wanted to stay. I know you tried to. I know you would if you could. Now I can't sleep because I can't stop thinking about you and how disappointed I feel that you're not here. My heart hurts. I don't understand why it hurts so much. I never used to think that longing for someone to be near, missing them so much, could actually cause physical pain. My heart hurts. It hurts to breathe. It hurts to move. It hurts to cry. It even hurts to touch my chest. I guess a heart really can break. And mine must be breaking. I have been having these feelings that are so confusing. Feelings I have never had before. Not even for Chris. I miss you like crazy right now. I miss your smell. I miss your face. I miss your smile. I miss your furrowed brow when you look at me from across a room. I miss the way my heart flutters when I see your face. The way I am feeling right now, the way I am missing you, I now know that I love you, Ryan, and I think I always have. Love isn't a big enough word to describe this paralyzing feeling that I have for you. And right now, I don't understand it. Maybe one day I will. Maybe one day I will be able to let you into my soul so that maybe you can feel how much I love you.

Ryan knew exactly what Larkin had meant.

His heart was broken, and he could feel the pain with every breath he took, with every toss and turn, with every word he spoke, with every step he took. The pain was still fresh, still seeping through every pore in his body. This letter touched him in a way that none of the others had. He had loved her back then, too, and he hadn't wanted to leave her. It killed him to leave her. If he had only known she had loved him, too, he would have never left.

He remembered that day when they took a walk in the park after her treatment. He hadn't told her yet that he had to go back to South Africa, and he couldn't stay with her that week. As they sat on the park bench together, he couldn't help but stare at her as her hair blew in the breeze. Despite what she had been through the past couple of months, he had thought she was more beautiful than ever. She was starting to lose her hair, and now she had to wear a wig. Her hair no longer rested past her shoulders. Instead, the wig fell just halfway between her neckline and shoulders, and the ends curled perfectly behind her ears. Her hair had been one length, but now she had bangs that swept across her forehead, complementing her heart-shaped face and her high cheekbones. She had rested her head on his shoulder, and he responded by putting his arm around her. As she rested her head on his shoulder, he proceeded to tell her about his inability to stay with her for the next three days and how his best friend Ian Marsico had offered to come stay with her until her parents came home. She never once took her head off his shoulder while he explained to her what was happening. He did take notice to the two times that she raised her hand up to her face to wipe her tears away, and each time he squeezed his arm around her a little tighter. She had never said a word. She had just nodded yes when he asked her if she was okay.

"I'm so sorry, Larkin. I really am. I would give anything to be able to stay. I don't want to be anywhere but here with you, I promise." Again, she had said nothing, and again she had raised her hand to her face to wipe her tears.

"Do you believe me, Larkin?" She had nodded yes, but her nod wasn't good enough for him. He had felt helpless and angry. He had wanted more than anything to be there with her, but he didn't know what else to do. He had actually felt himself feeling jealous that Ian was going to be there instead of him.

Ryan guided Larkin up off the bench and back to the car. They had a two-hour ride ahead of them back to Somers Point. The clouds began to break even more, and the sun's rays were getting warmer and warmer. Larkin still had not said much to Ryan since he told her he was not staying. The traffic was light on the normally jam-packed Atlantic City Expressway, so they were making good time. Halfway through the trip, Larkin had pulled out her manuscript and started to read from where she had finished when they drove to the hospital earlier in the day. As she had begun to read, Ryan had breathed a sigh of relief. She was reading to him, and that was a sign she was okay. More importantly, that was a sign *they were* okay.

Ryan went to Los Angeles in 1995 when he was nineteen years old with very little money in his pocket and no contacts. He had built his career from scratch with a lot of good looks, a lot of talent, and a little bit of luck. He caught his first break when he met Ian Marsico, who was twenty-four at the time and who had already made a name for himself in Hollywood. Ian took a quick liking to Ryan and subsequently took him under his wing. He saw Ryan's potential and introduced him to the right people. It was shortly after that Ryan had landed a small role in a feature film, and his career took off soon after. Ryan has never forgotten what Ian has done for him, and he never will. They became the best of friends with each being the other's best man at their weddings, and they never missed one another's premieres. And it was Ian who Ryan turned to when he first learned of Larkin's sickness. Ian would know the right things to say, and he would always be able to put things in perspective for him.

When Leon had told Ryan he could only have two days instead of the previously agreed upon four days for Larkin's treatment, the only person he could think of to call was Ian. Ian and Larkin had become fast friends when Ryan first introduced them to each other, and the three of them had spent a lot of time together whenever Larkin would come visit. Ian had even called Larkin a couple of times, checking on her after she got sick. Ryan knew she had liked and trusted Ian, so he knew that it was going to be okay that he was coming to stay with her, at least he had hoped.

Letter #13 - October 18, 2011

Hey, lovely,

Ian got here last night, as you know. I have always liked him. He has been a good friend to you, and I know he has your back. I always thought of him as dark and handsome. I can't say tall, dark, and handsome (what is he? 5'10, 5'11?) but dark and handsome with his dark brown hair, dark brown eyes, and dark tan skin. His dimples complement his wide smile that seems to stretch from ear to ear, and one thing I love about him is that he never tries to dress to impress. He had long black jeans on with holes in both knees, and his black flip-flops just barely peaked out from underneath the fraying ends of his pants. His faded white and blue Yankees long-sleeved T-shirt was partially covered by a black leather jacket, and his curly, messy hair was hidden by a Yankees cap. By the way, we need to talk to him about his choice in baseball teams! Another thing I love about him is that he is still happily married after eight years. I love his family, Linda and their beautiful children, Jack and Isabella. He gives me hope for you, Ryan. If he can figure out how to make a Hollywood marriage last, you can, too. He flashed his Hollywood smile toward me as I let him in, and he dropped his bags so he could embrace me. He has always been nice to me. You have good taste in friends, Ryan (*wink, wink*).

Much to my disapproval, Ian didn't want to impose on my sister's room (even though she hasn't lived there in nearly a decade), and he elected to sleep on the couch. After he finally got settled in, the three of us sat around the fireplace in the family room for nearly two hours catching up on the past several months. It was a great night, and I could tell you were happy to see him. I don't remember falling asleep, but Ian told me how you carried me to my bedroom. The last thing I remember is sitting next to you with my head on your shoulder. I remember the occasional stroke of your hand upon my forehead, brushing the bangs out of my eyes, the frequent rubbing of my arm that rested across your chest, and the subtle kisses on the top of my head...

Ryan remembered joining Ian on the porch that night after he took Larkin upstairs. It was killing him to leave her there, especially knowing how sick she got after the first chemo treatment. Ryan had called Ian several times to vent his frustration about her illness so he knew Ian was aware of how he was feeling.

"Call me if anything happens. Anything..."

"Ryan." Ian cut him off. "Relax. Everything will be fine. I promise you, I will take care of her. What could possibly happen?"

"I don't know..." His voice trailed off. He was fighting to keep control. "She hasn't said much to me since I told her I couldn't stay. I hate leaving knowing she's upset."

"Look, I'll have her call you when she wakes up in the morning. You two can talk then.

Until then, relax, have a safe trip, and get some rest. I will take care of her. You don't need to worry about a thing.'

The old friends exchanged a quick handshake as Ryan's cab pulled up to take him to Atlantic City International for his red-eye flight back to Cape Town.

He continued reading the letter.

...I fell last night trying to get to the bathroom. I must have really scared Ian because he ran up here so fast. I heard him stumble as he ran up the stairs. Thankfully, you left me a bucket at the side of the bed so I was able to reach for that. I would have felt awful if Ian would have had to clean up my vomit. When he realized I was okay, he helped me stand up and steered me to the bed as I held on tightly to his arms. I sat on the edge of the bed waiting as he brought me a wet towel to wash my face and hands.

He asked me if I had hurt myself. He was a trooper, Ryan. He never cringed from the smell of the vomit or looked away from my face that probably had some left on it. You would be proud. I could tell he was concerned. I was too exhausted to even speak, so I just nodded my head to assure him I had not hurt myself. He told me he didn't feel comfortable leaving me alone, so after he went back downstairs to grab his pillow and blankets, he laid next to me for the next several hours until I awoke.

I didn't feel well enough to eat anything, but Ian was able to talk me into coming downstairs with him as he ate lunch. He carried me to the recliner because I could barely walk, and we watched movies from noon until dinnertime. I had gotten sick several times, but I always felt a little bit better afterward. He would sneak out onto the front porch to smoke whenever he thought I fell asleep. The one time, I heard him on the phone with Linda, and the other time I heard him talking to you. When he came back in, he noticed I was awake and told me you called to check on me.

I miss you, Ryan. I don't mind Ian being here, but I miss you. I want you here. I want to tell you how much I love and need you.

Ryan will never forget the first time Larkin told him she loved him.

Love. He was doing it for love. It had to be the reason. It was the only logical reason. Why else would he have sacrificed his career to be by her side? They had been three quarters of the way done with the movie. They were finally ahead of schedule. Leon could do without him for a couple more days. But of course, he wouldn't see it that way. He had wanted Ryan there and nowhere else. He was a control freak, and he wanted to control his cast and his crew. He had told Ryan, "You're lucky I let you have two days away." He wasn't too terrible to work with. Sure, he had them work twelve-to sixteen-hour days, but he was good about giving actors two days off a week. He just didn't want them leaving the country, especially his lead actor. Besides, Leon was one of the most successful directors in Hollywood, and every actor aspired to work under him. Ryan had done everything Leon had asked of him.

But that time was different. How could he expect Leon to understand? Leon had never been in love. He had three children from three different women. He had never married, and he had a different woman on his arm at all his red carpet events. Ryan had been worried. He had only texted Leon to tell him he was leaving for the rest of the week. He didn't even tell him face-to-face. He knew Leon would have given him an ultimatum. But at that time, he just didn't care. At that point, he was willing to sacrifice his career to be by Larkin's side. He hadn't known how sick she really was, so he hadn't known if she would even live much longer. And he was going to be there with her every step of the way, even if he had to bring her back to South Africa with him.

He had caught the red-eye out of Cape Town, just two hours after he talked to Ian that night. He would be in Atlantic City in sixteen hours. He had hoped to be in Somers Point by noon. *Thank God for the time change*, he thought.

Ryan had fallen asleep in the cab on the way to Larkin's. He was so jetlagged. He had had a headache for two days, and his sleep patterns were so out of whack his body didn't know if it should be asleep or awake. His body was so disoriented. He had been on two sixteen-hour flights in a matter of two days, and he would have been just fine with it if he never had to get back on an airplane again.

The cab pulled up in front of Larkin's house, and he had seen Ian smoking on the front porch. He hadn't told Ian he was coming, so he knew he would be more than surprised. As he made his way down the slate walkway connecting the driveway to the porch, Ian stood up and extended his hand to greet him. Ian never said a word to him; he just gave him a nod and tilted his head toward the second floor, signaling to Ryan that Larkin was resting upstairs.

Ryan had placed his luggage on the floor at the base of Larkin's bed. She was sleeping, and he could see the bucket next to her bed was half full of vomit. He, without thinking twice, had picked the bucket up and emptied it into the bathroom toilet, cleaned it with soap and water, and quietly placed it back next to her bed. He stripped down to his boxers and tank-top shirt and quietly slipped in under the covers next to her. He had noticed her cheek and the side of her nose was damp, and a small tear was stuck in the corner of her eye. He gently wiped it away with his finger, taking notice of the subtle curve of her cheekbone and the light pink color of her lips. As she opened her eyes and realized him lying there next to her, she buried her face in his chest and began to cry. Her breaths were deep and shallow, and he could tell she was having a hard time breathing. He gently lifted her chin up so he could see her face.

"Larkin, breathe. Take a deep breath."

She slowly started to calm down, catching her breath. "Larkin, I'm here. It's okay. What's going on? What's wrong?"

"Ryan." She paused for a moment. He never took his gaze off her eyes.

"Ryan, I love you. I love you so much, I can't breathe when you're gone." She buried her face back into his chest. He knew it had taken everything she had to tell him that. She had risked ruining their friendship by telling him. He knew because that was exactly the way he had felt. He had wanted to tell her for the past month that he loved her, but he couldn't. He didn't know how she would have reacted, and he would never risk their friendship. But now he knew. She felt the same way.

Again, he pulled her chin up, guiding her face up to his so he could look into her blue eyes. "Then take *my* breath. I'll be your breath when you can't breathe." And with that, he pressed his slightly opened lips against hers, cradling her face with his hands, allowing her to breathe him in. He held his lips against hers until she calmed down, and then he slowly pulled away. He wiped her tears away.

"Kiss me, Larkin, anytime you can't breathe, anytime you want to cry, you kiss me. You hear me?"

She nodded.

"Close your eyes, Lark. I promise I will be here when you open them."

Her eyelids slowly fell, covering her tear-filled eyes, and as her mind and her body and her sickness drifted off into sleep, Ryan closed his eyes and pressed his lips against hers again, never taking them away until his eyes opened several hours later. Ryan remembered that next week like it was yesterday. That week with her had been an awakening for him, an awakening of his feelings for Larkin, an awakening of how important she was to him, an awakening of his hopes for the future with her. Although she had been recovering from the chemo treatment, he enjoyed the time he had spent with her. He had held her every night in his arms, and he would listen to the beating of her heart and her breaths as she would drift away into sleep. He had cooked for her, and they would hold hands across the table as they ate, and they watched movies every night—their favorite movies from childhood. When she had started to feel stronger, they would take the long walk hand-in-hand down to the pier, and they would sit together at the edge watching the fish swim by. They would watch the boats throughout the bay—some anchored, others drifting—as fishermen were trying to conquer that last keeper of the season. Sometimes, if it wasn't too crowded, they would sit on the beach together, Ryan embracing her as she sat in front of him, and he would gently brush her hair out of her eyes when the breeze from the ocean water would graze her face. As they talked about life, she would frequently rest the back of her head against his shoulder, close her eyes, and tell him she loved him. And each time, he would hold her a little tighter and sweep her cheek with his lips. He remembers they had seen an elderly couple walking hand-in-hand down the beach and Larkin had asked Ryan, "Do you think that will be us one day?"

"God, I hope so" was all he could say. And all he *could* do was hope.

Those had been the best moments that he had experienced in a long time. He hadn't wanted them to end, but it was hard to ignore the life that had been waiting for him back in Cape Town. But when he was with Larkin, he had felt like he was in a completely different life, a life that he had left behind when he had moved away fifteen years ago. He had wished that he had never left. The miles had torn them worlds apart, and he had wished he could have had those fifteen years back, fifteen years he could have had with her. He had loved the life he had been living, but he had finally come to the realization that he had loved her more.

Letter #14 - October 24, 2011

Dear Ryan,

You're going back to South Africa tomorrow, and I am going to miss you so much. Even though I am fighting for my life right now, I have never felt more alive. This week has been so many things to me: extraordinary, confusing, uplifting, and magical. We fell in love this past week. I think my heart fell for you a long time ago, but now you have finally caught it. And I know you will nurture it, and you'll never let it go. You do so much just to make me smile, and I promise you I am going to do everything I can to make you smile.

Most people will make small sacrifices in life, usually for their own gain. But a true sacrifice is giving up your own happiness in order to make someone else happy. How many people have come across your path in life and made a sacrifice for you so enormous, it took your breath away? Most people would probably say no one. I, on the other hand, am one of the lucky ones. I am lucky because, Ryan, you are the epitome of what sacrifice is all about. And what makes you so extraordinary is that you didn't make just one sacrifice, you made numerous. You are sacrificing your career, your time, your desires, your money and humility, all for me. I ask myself why every day. I can only hope that you fully understand how grateful and indebted I will always feel to you. I don't know if it is possible to find the words to explain to you all that you have been to me. Ryan, you are so good to me. Why are you so good to me?

CHAPTER 7

Letter #15 - December 26, 2011

My Ryan,

I haven't written to you in a while because we have been inseparable these past several weeks. But even though we are spending more time together, I still want to write to you to let you know my thoughts and my feelings. Even though we are going to share almost everything from here on out, I still want you to be able to remember. Remembering the good things will help you heal.

As the warm, autumn breeze slowly transitioned to harsh cold winds, the treetops that were once dressed in reds and oranges are now blanketed with winter's snow. The normal hustle and bustle of the summer and early fall—the neighborhood kids playing in the streets, tourists traveling by foot to the beaches, the procession of pick-up trucks and SUVs at the docks waiting to launch their boats and Jet Skis into the Great Egg Harbor Bay, the jam-packed boardwalks, the lines at the amusement rides, the sky littered with parasailers and small airplanes pulling banners advertising the local seafood restaurants—had all come to a sudden halt as early winter had cast its unwelcoming spell over Somers Point and the surrounding ocean towns, turning them into ghost towns. I had my third treatment on the second Monday in November—ten days before Thanksgiving—and after celebrating an early holiday dinner with my parents, we flew to Cape Town together where you were going to finally be wrapping your movie. You vowed never to leave me again after my treatments, and you were going to do everything you could to make sure you were by my side.

We spent the next four weeks in Cape Town before we had to come back for my fourth treatment, but it was a quick trip, and we headed right back to Cape Town so you could wrap your film. You were so busy with work, but you tried your best to show me what Cape Town had to offer. You took me to the Atlantic Seaboard, Blaauwberg Coast, and to Cape Flats. We hiked. We fished. We biked. We swam. We did everything we had time for. Even though you wrapped the movie a week before Christmas, we decided to spend Christmas together in Cape Town, and it was amazing. You got permission from the hotel and surprised me with a tree, and we spent Christmas Eve decorating it, taking several breaks to enjoy a dance together to the slow beat of the Christmas music. And you surprised me on Christmas morning with an amazing gift: a white gold heart-shaped locket with a picture of us inside. I don't want to leave here. I love it, and I love you, and while I was here, leukemia never crossed my mind. Just you. Just you on my mind. Just you and me together. Nothing is better.

Now we are traveling back to New Jersey to finish my treatments. We are into the tenth hour on this more than half a day plane ride across the world. In between sentences, I frequently glance down at your perfect face as you sleep next to me, your head on my shoulder. I am overwhelmed by the way you make me feel. I can't believe you love me. Me.

You were supposed to start filming another movie in two months, but you have decided you are going to take a hiatus from acting. You are truly amazing, and the sacrifices you have been making for me are humbling, and I don't know what to make of it. I ask again, Ryan. Why are you so good to me?

His time with Larkin in South Africa back then had only solidified his feelings for her, and he was going to spend every moment he could with her. Christmastime had given way to the New Year, and Larkin had finished her sixth and final treatment by February's end. The chemo treatments had taken almost everything out of her, and although she did everything she was told to do by the doctors, her body had been through a war. In six weeks, they would find out if the chemo was working. Ryan had taken as good of care as he could have of Larkin, and with each day's passing, they fell more and more in love. Ryan had rented a house with a private dock that sat nestled among the bay homes outlining the lagoons in Ocean City, and they stayed there together. He had missed the warm sunny days that Los Angeles had to offer especially at this time of year, but he knew he had made the right decision. As much as he loved acting and making movies, every morning when he had woken up next to Larkin, he had never felt happier. That was where he was supposed to be at that moment in his life.

Letter #16 – March 10, 2012

Dear Ryan,

Signs of springtime are creeping upon the Jersey Shore and along with the birth and new life of flower blooms and tree buds comes hope for my recovery. Birdsong is slowly making a comeback, offering sweet morning serenades from the treetops that sit just outside our bedroom window. We are playing a waiting game, and it will be six more weeks before we find out if the cancer is gone. I spend much of my time trying to finish my manuscript, which is why I haven't written to you in a while, and you spend your mornings on the water fishing on your newly purchased Grady White. You always make a daily stop at the flower shop, picking out a different bouquet each time to bring home to me. You are still so good to me. It is still too cold for me to join you on your morning fishing trips. My immune system is still compromised, and I cannot take a chance of getting sick. The slightest cold could easily turn into pneumonia, and that is not a battle we are willing to fight. But I would give anything to be out on that boat with you.

I want to write to you about yesterday. Yesterday was a great day. I want you to remember it like I do. Like you do every afternoon when you dock, you hosed down the boat, making sure to clean off the saltwater. You smiled at me when you noticed me watching you while I read on our back deck. Over the past several days, I knew you could tell that I hadn't fully recovered from the last chemo treatment, but I think after you saw me on the deck reading, you knew I must have been feeling better. I could see the relief in your smile. I took a minute to watch you as you cleaned off the boat. You are so meticulous with the way you clean up that boat. Just like how you take care of me. Your beauty is vast, limitless, and cosmic. You have no idea how beautiful you are, and that makes you even more beautiful. After you finished, you made your way up the stairs that connected the deck to the dock, and as I looked up at you away from my book, you brought flowers out from behind your back.

"They get more beautiful each day," I said, reaching out my hand to grab them.

"Just like you," you responded, kissing me on the forehead.

"I caught us some dinner today," you proudly said as you made your way through the

sliding glass door into the house to wash your hands.

"Did you really? Well, if you fillet them, I'll cook them."

You were quick to accept that deal. "You look like you are feeling better today!" you shouted from inside.

"Yeah, I am actually. I wasn't as tired when I woke up this morning."

You made your way back onto the deck and knelt before me. "Well, then, are you up for some dancing after dinner tonight?"

"I would love it, Ryan." We shared a long kiss before you retired to the shower.

You had caught two twenty-inch flounders on your morning fishing trip, and after you filleted them, you threw them on the grill while I prepared the side dishes. I had originally wanted to bake the fish, but you insisted that you grill them instead. We enjoyed a banquet with all the food I had prepared, and of course, there were leftovers, as always. You always say to me, "Larkin, it's just the two of us. You don't need to make so much food." But cooking is a newfound interest for me. I did very little of it when I was married to Chris, but now I have been doing it more and more since I am at home all the time.

After I put the leftovers away, I started cleaning up the dishes. I could hear you fumbling around with something in the family room, and as soon as I closed the dishwasher door and pressed start, music could be heard over the surround system. I turned around and saw you standing there as you held out your hand for me.

"Dance with me?" you asked.

"What, here?" I thought that when you had asked me to go dancing, you meant go out dancing.

"Yeah, here. Why not?"

I approached your 6'2" frame, and as my hand fell into yours, you spun me around and guided me into a perfect slow dance. Dancing with you offers me a peace that I have never experienced before. When you hold me close, I feel as if everything is right in the world and that nothing can touch me. Not even leukemia. I have always loved you, and I knew that, but it wasn't until the past six months that I have realized just how much. I didn't think it was possible to love another human being the way I love you. It is almost frightening to me. I have never felt so vulnerable, as weak, to another as I do to you. Dancing with you gives me hope. Hope for a future with you. Hope that my disease will be cured, and I can give everything I am to you. Hope is all I have. Hope is the foundation for my strength.

As we danced, I took in your scent. I always loved the way you smell—clean and musky, seductive and sensual. Your scent is intoxicating and addicting, and I didn't want to let go of you. You would frequently spin me away from you, and you would stare into my eyes as we swayed together to the sweet strings of the orchestra that emitted out of the radio speakers. You move like water. You have turned into a great dancer, Ryan. I was in heaven. Maybe I have already died and gone to heaven. You are my angel, my light at the end of the tunnel. You are my warmth, my peace, my strength, my hope. You are everything I have always thought of as heaven being.

I still can't believe you have taken time off your career to be with me. I feel bad that you don't get to see your friends and that you have put off a major movie production to be with me. I begged you not to. But you didn't want to hear any of it. You promised me that this was what you wanted and that this is where you are supposed to be at this exact moment in your life. "Acting will always be there. You may not," you would plead to me. Although it is an awful thing to say, you are right. Neither of us knows what the future is.

My knees were starting to weaken from the dancing, and once you realized that you were the only thing holding me up, you carried me to the patio recliner on the back deck. You went inside to grab a blanket to wrap us up in as you held me while we listened to the tide come in. "Thanks for the dance," you whispered in my ear. I leaned my head against your chest, and I was so overwhelmed with the feelings that you had ignited inside of me. I absorbed the surroundings. As we sat in silence, I watched as the last of the Jet Skis and boats weaved their way into the lagoons to dock before the last of the sun went down. The warm season is just getting started, and this has always been my favorite time of the year—the tourist season. I love the excitement that exudes from parents as they watch their young children experience the sand and the ocean for the first time. I love watching teenagers experience the excitement of their first big catch as their fathers help them reel it inside the boat. I love watching couples walk hand-in- hand or arm-in-arm where the water meets the sand, letting all their troubles go, if only for that moment. This is a place where people come to get away, to create happy memories, and to try to forget about the bad ones. It's humbling to know that our home is really a sanctuary for most other people. But for me, my sanctuary is in your arms and nowhere else.

"What are you thinking about?" You broke the silence as you held me close to keep me warm.

"I was thinking about how much you mean to me," I answered.

"Oh yeah? How much?"

I buried my head into your chest, trying to become one with your heart.

"I'm dying," I paused for a moment. "I'm dying, and the most valuable thing to me, right now, is my life. But somehow still, I seem to love you more than I love my life. And I don't want to keep on fighting to live if I can't live without you."

You lifted my chin so that my eyes could meet yours. "Well, then, keep on fighting, baby, because you will never have to live without me."

"You promise?"

"I promise." And with that, you stood up with me out of the recliner with my legs wrapped around your waist. As you wrapped the blanket around me, you kissed me like you never kissed me before. For just a moment, you released our kiss. "I love you, Larkin. Let me take you to a place you have never been before." And as you kissed me again, you carried me into the house and up the stairs to our bedroom where we made love for the first time.

I took notice of the gentle way you had taken care not to hurt my fragile body, and you never took your eyes away from mine. I let you take me to that place that you had promised, and you took my breath away, and you made me feel like a woman. I suddenly knew at that moment that you are my heaven, and I was in awe of this beautiful angel that had placed his body on top of mine. You are strong and masculine, but you took care of me the way a man should take care of a woman he loves. After I caught my breath, I raised my hand up to your face, brushing your flushed cheekbone before I outlined your lips with the tip of my finger.

"Take me there again," I pleaded with you. As the sun set and the moon took its place, as the stars gave cover to the chilly March evening, throughout the night, you and I repeatedly became as close as a man and a woman can become. And just before the sun rose the next morning, you watched as I let myself go to that magical place that you had taken me so many times that night, a place

that you too had gone with me. As I returned back to you, out of breath, you caressed my forehead with your hand, your brown eyes staring into mine. You gently kissed my nose, and you decided to give all of yourself to me at that moment.

"Marry me, Larkin," you whispered.

Letter #17 – March 10, 2012

Hey, Fish,

It has been the typical morning that we have become accustomed to. You on your daily fishing trip and me typing away on my manuscript. But it isn't typical, really. We had shared a magical night together, a night that strengthened and solidified what we have meant to each other, and from this morning forward, our lives will never be the same. I have a feeling of excitement for the first time in a long time. For the first time since I have gotten sick, I have a powerful sense of optimism. There is something inside of me that you have set off that has made me feel stronger than ever. But I have to admit to you that I am also a little worried. Worried that maybe you didn't mean what you had said when you asked me to marry you. I never really did give you an answer. I just kissed you like I had never kissed you before right after you said it. Even though I didn't acknowledge your impulsive proposal, I certainly haven't forgotten it. I just hope that you meant it and that you weren't caught up in the moment. But I am nervous. I'm not even sure if I would be doing right by you to marry you. You deserve a lifetime of love, and I cannot promise you that.

I am writing you a second letter today because I need to find a way to cope with what happened after you got back today. I know you told me I have nothing to worry about, but you know me. After you got back from your fishing trip, we sat over a cup of coffee before you went to the shower. Neither of us mentioned what happened last night. Although it was the best night of my life, I am scared that maybe you have some regrets. It is so hard for me not to talk to you about it and find out how you are feeling about what happened and most importantly about what you asked me, but I have decided that I am going to give you your space and let you come to me about it. I am not going to push you.

I decided that I would try to let my mind escape from these thoughts by delving into a novel as you showered and got cleaned up. My mind, half-focused on the novel and half-focused on last night, was unexpectedly interrupted by a knock on our door. I know that I wasn't expecting anyone and you hadn't mentioned that you were, so I figured it was a neighbor or just my mother paying us an unannounced visit. I never in a million years expected to see the face that was staring back at me as I opened the door. I can only imagine what my face must have looked like to her as I struggled to even say hello. Finally, she broke the awkward silence.

"Hi Larkin," she paused, probably expecting me to say something back, but, again, I couldn't find the words to replace my shock at seeing her. She smiled, looking more beautiful than I remembered. "You look really good, Larkin. How are you?"

"Good," I paused. "I'm good. Thanks. You look good, too, as always."

She leaned forward, and we embraced in a very awkward hug. My heart was inevitably sinking as I finally found the courage to invite her in.

"Come in, Abigail. I'll let Ryan know you're here."

I truly believe that timing really is everything. I would be lying to you, Ryan, if I told you that I wasn't worried about Abigail being here. Why is she here? Is it really just an innocent visit like you tried to reassure me before you two went out to go talk over lunch? Or is it more? Maybe not for you, but for her. Maybe she wants you back. Why wouldn't you want to go back if she did? I could never give you what she can. She's beautiful, healthy, and successful. She's everything you deserve, and I know how much you loved her when you were with her. I know how heartbroken you were when it ended. I know that as I watch you sleep next to me as I write this. Tonight was the first night you didn't hold me as I fell asleep. You just kissed my nose, wished me sweet dreams, and rolled over. You have been different since you returned from your visit with her. I am sure you are just as surprised as I am that she came. Maybe you're just coping with the shock, too. Maybe, just maybe, it really was innocent and everything is going to be okay. Or maybe you don't know how to hurt me. It's not in your nature to hurt me. I know that I love you more than anything and no matter what happens I always will.

CHAPTER 8

Ryan didn't try to, but he had shut Larkin out when Abigail came back into his life. He had tried to fight the urge to allow Abigail back into his life, but he had always had a soft spot for her. Seeing her had brought him back to the life he had left; a life that he loved living. He knew he eventually would have gotten back to that life, but seeing Abigail that day had tempted him to go back to it sooner rather than later.

He remembers seeing Abigail sitting on the couch as he made his way down the stairs. He wasn't expecting to see her. Larkin had only come up to tell him someone was there to see him, but she didn't say who.

"Abby?" he said. "What are you doing here?"

"Hi, Ryan." She smiled as she stood up to greet him. Her smile had always made him melt. "I was in New York for an event, so I thought I would come down to see you. I stopped by your mother's house, but she told me you lived here now. I hope it's okay I am here."

"It's okay." He couldn't take his eyes off her. She was still so beautiful. "You look great, Abby."

"I was wondering if we could talk. Do you have time? I was thinking maybe we could grab some lunch."

He glanced over to Larkin. "Well, Larkin and I were getting ready to go out for lunch."

"It's okay, Ryan. You two go and catch up. I'll be okay. There's plenty to eat here," Larkin said.

He approached her and grabbed her shoulders. "Are you sure?"

Larkin nodded with an uneasy smile. He could see she was doing her best to not let him see the apprehension in her eyes.

"Larkin, I don't have to go."

"No, no, I want you to. It will be good for you to see an old friend."

He studied her face for a moment before deciding that he would go. "Okay. I won't be long." He kissed her on the forehead. "I promise."

Ryan drove Abigail a couple of blocks away to a local diner, and they sat in the far side corner so no one would recognize them. More so for Abigail's privacy as the locals had started to get used to seeing Ryan around town. The conversation over lunch had been slow and awkward as they both struggled getting used to being in each other's presence again. The divorce had been amicable for the most part, but Ryan had wanted to work a little harder at making it work. He still held some resentment toward Abigail for not trying harder. They decided to order coffee after they finished lunch. As they waited, Abigail reached across the table and grabbed Ryan's hand. As much as he knew he should pull away from her delicate grasp, he couldn't bring himself to. Instead, he brushed his thumb across her fingers and locked his eyes with her. He felt like he had been transported back to two years ago when they were happy and in love. But when Abigail finally spoke, the words she had said brought him back to reality, and he quickly pulled his hand away from hers.

"I miss you, Ryan," she said.

At that moment, Ryan knew she had come to see him for reasons other than just catching up.

"What do you want me to say to that, Abigail?" Those words had made him angry. *I miss you? After all this time? Where were you when I wanted to make it work? You left. You gave up.* These thoughts consumed his mind, but he couldn't seem to form them into words.

"I don't know, Ryan. Maybe you miss me too?" He could hear the desperation in her voice.

"I did miss you, Abby. I couldn't sleep. I couldn't eat. I wanted us to work. But you gave up. So, again, what am I supposed to say to that?"

"I'm sorry, Ryan. I am. But I realized I

made the biggest mistake of my life after I left. I didn't realize what I had until you were gone. I still love you."

I still love you. Those were the words Ryan had been longing to hear from Abigail for so long after their divorce. But it was too late. She had waited too long. *Why is she doing this? Why now? I have finally been able to move on, and now she comes back into my life.* Ryan tried to make sense of what was happening.

Abigail interrupted his thoughts. "Don't you remember when you handed me the signed divorce papers you told me you would always love me?"

Ryan did remember, but he didn't want to. He was afraid he still might. "Abigail...I can't leave Larkin."

"Ryan, you have been an amazing friend to her. You have gone above and beyond what friends do for each other. But you have given up everything for her. You have sacrificed your career and your friends. She isn't alone. She has her family and her friends. And if she is your best friend, she would want you to be happy. You can't let her hold you back from your life anymore. You need to come home. Come back to work."

"Abby, she is not holding me back. I am choosing to be here with her."

"Well, then choose to let her go. Choose to follow your heart. And if it is still with me, then you need to follow it and finally do something for yourself."

All Ryan could think about was the night he had shared with Larkin, but he couldn't bring himself to tell Abigail. He was scared to tell her that he and Larkin had fallen in love. He couldn't understand why he was so scared to tell her. Perhaps he didn't want to hurt her feelings. Or maybe it was...and he was afraid to even understand this...but maybe it was because he did still love Abigail and he didn't want her to know what had happened between him and Larkin. Ryan did love Larkin. He had fallen in love with her. But seeing Abigail again and hearing her say that she still loved him had unburied the feelings he had once felt for her. Maybe Abigail was right. Maybe his loyalty to Larkin was holding him back. It wasn't Larkin's fault, of course. She had never asked him for anything. But he had always been a loyal man, and sometimes loyalty can hold you back from the things you truly desire.

Ryan drove Abigail back to his house, and as they shared a good-bye embrace, she had whispered in his ear, "Follow your heart, Ryan. Come home. Even if it's not to me, at least come home."

Letter #18 - March 12, 2012

Ryan,

Today was a tough day for me. It hurts me to even write about it, let alone remind you of it. It is definitely not one of the best memories we have shared. The past two days I have watched you as you slowly drift away from me. It has been almost two days since Abigail has come to see you. And just like I wrote in my last letter, since you came home from your visit with her, you have been different. You are still kind and attentive toward my needs, but your eyes are a million miles away. Every time I ask you if you're okay, you tell me you are, and you then you kiss my forehead. But it is hard for me to believe that everything is okay because ever since Abigail left, you have not told me you love me, and you have not kissed me on my lips.

I can't believe I did what I did this morning, but I just couldn't bear to see you drift away from me any further. I know our friendship has evolved into an amazing love affair, but I can't bear to not have you in my life. If that means that I need to let you go just so we can salvage our friendship, then I need to let you go.

I wouldn't be a good friend if I didn't push you to follow your dreams and your heart, and if I am not or cannot be a part of your dreams, then I need to set you free.

Thank you for being so good to me.

This last letter reminded Ryan that he did not deserve Larkin. She was right. The reminder of this day was painful to relive. He had come home from fishing that morning and greeted Larkin in the kitchen with a hug. Her hug was distant and cold, and he had noticed over her shoulder a luggage bag sitting in front of the door. "What's this, Larkin?" he asked nodding his head towards the bag.

She was silent as she looked down, not able to look at him in the eyes. He tilted her chin up, forcing her to look at him, and he could see her fighting back the tears. "What's with the bag, Larkin?"

"I'm going home to my parents," she said, her voice almost a whisper.

"Why? This is your home."

"No," she replied shaking her head, "no, it's not. You haven't truly been here since Abigail came to see you. I don't know where your mind is, although I have an idea, and I can't handle watching you as you continue to drift away. And it's not fair for me to make you feel like you have to stay."

"You don't make me feel like I have to stay. I want to be here."

"I know you want to help me, and you have, Ryan. But now it is time for me to let you go. You're different since she left. You haven't told me you love me, you don't kiss me, and you know what? It's okay. It's okay if you want to go back to her. I know how much you loved her. She can give you so much more than I ever could. Don't worry about me. I have my family and friends. Go live your life. The life you have dreamed of."

Ryan pulled Larkin in close to him. "Larkin, we are living. And I am sorry if I have been distant lately. I'm not going to lie to you. I have been thinking about Abby the past few days, but I do love you, and I don't want you to think that I don't. And I don't want you to think that I am going to leave you."

"No, Ryan, we're not living. We're surviving. And I know you love me, but we fell in love in the shadow of my sickness. If I never would have gotten sick, we would have never fallen in love, and you would go back to Abigail." She could no longer hold her tears in.

"I am going to go back to work. I just want to know you will be okay. We find out in a few weeks."

"And if I'm not okay? Then what? Then you stay? Trapped in the confines of my sickness."

"That's not the case, Larkin. I'm not trapped."

"Can you honestly stand here and look me in the eyes and tell me that you don't still love her? That seeing her again hasn't sparked something inside of you?" All Ryan could do was look down and say nothing. He honestly didn't know what he was feeling at that moment.

Larkin brushed Ryan's cheek with her fingers. "Ryan, you are such a good man. I know you don't want to hurt me. I know you want to be here for me. But I am going to be okay. I'm a big girl. I want you to go live the life you have dreamed of." Her words were abruptly interrupted by the sound of a car horn in the driveway.

"I need to go. That's my ride."

"Larkin…the other night."

"Ryan, it's okay. It was a great night. We were caught up in the moment," her voice cracked as she held back from crying. He couldn't bear to see her cry.

She wrapped her arms around him. "You will always be my best friend. You will always be my fish. Thank you for being so good to me." She quickly pulled from their embrace, turned away without even looking at him, grabbed her bag, and walked out the door leaving him only with the scent of her perfume to hold on to.

Two days later, Ryan showed up at Abigail's doorstep in Los Angeles. He wasn't sure if he was doing the right thing, but he needed to find out. He had hated leaving Larkin behind, but he had to find out if the love he had felt for her was real or if he did indeed belong with Abigail. His goodbye with Larkin and her tears haunted him at night. He didn't feel as if he said all that was needed to say to her. He felt as if he left her without a care in the world, as if the night they had shared didn't mean anything to him. It had meant something to him, but he wasn't sure if it meant more than his past with Abigail. When Abigail opened the door, her beauty took his breath away. She was stunned to see him standing there. All he could do was smile at her. She reached out and pulled him into her arms and whispered into his ear, "Welcome home, Ryan."

It took Ryan a few days to feel comfortable

with Abigail again. He held her at a safe distance; after all, she had broken his trust when she left him. She was busy filming during the day, and he had set up a couple of meetings with his agent to discuss future projects, so they didn't see each other much except in the evenings. The time they did spend together was easy. It was as if they picked up right where they left off, especially when they kissed for the first time in years as they cuddled on the living room floor next to the fireplace. Ryan had started to finally begin to feel like maybe he did belong with her. She was different than before. She seemed committed this time around to making them work.

There was never a day he didn't think about Larkin. He had found himself starting to dial her number but always hung up midway through. He had no idea what he would say to her. He wondered if she was still feeling well or if her health was starting to decline again. He couldn't bear to think she was sick again and he had left her alone. All he could do was hope she would call him if she needed him. But something told him she wouldn't. He felt as if he had lost her forever. His best friend. His lullaby. His blue eyes. She was gone.

CHAPTER 9

Letter #19 - April 8, 2012

Dear Ryan,

I don't know why, but I have decided to keep writing to you. I know we have gone our separate ways, but I meant it when I said you will always be my best friend. I am going to continue to write to you just so you never forget that you are the most important person in my life. I want you to know how I am doing. One day I will send you these letters. When the time is right.

I am still feeling pretty good. It is only a couple of more weeks until I find out if the chemotherapy worked. I would be lying to you if I told you I wasn't scared. I'm terrified.

I would also be lying to you if I told you I didn't miss you. That I wish I hadn't left that day. That maybe you do really love me and I was stupid for pushing you away. But I was watching the awards ceremony on TV tonight, and I saw you on the red carpet with Abigail. You were smiling and holding her hand. You looked so happy. You looked free. You were where you belong. That's when I realized I had made the right decision. That you had made the right decision.

I am happy for you, Ryan. I am happy that you are free. Free from the obligation that you feel towards me. Free from the strangling grasp of my sickness.

Now it's time for you to fly.

As Ryan finished reading this letter, he realized how wrong Larkin had been. He wasn't happy. He wasn't free. It had all been an act. An act for the cameras. The two weeks prior to that awards ceremony had not been all that great, at least for him. Abigail had started to feel comfortable again with him. She was back to her old habits. He had started to see that it was more important to her to be seen with him than it was to actually be with him. She wanted him to be by her side for every event she needed to attend, but when they had free time to spend together, she would rather go out to parties with her friends. He was essentially her arm candy.

The night of the awards ceremony was a revelation for Ryan. He had started to realize what type of person she really was when he saw how she would flaunt him in front of the cameras and hear some of the comments she made to fellow actors, especially the comment she made when a fellow actress had made a remark about how it was nice seeing them back together again.

"Yes, it is great. He finally has his priorities straight," she had replied.

That comment had angered him. *Priorities? Aren't you the one who left me in the first place? Where were your priorities?* He couldn't believe how she couldn't understand that helping his best friend in need, a friend who was fighting for her life no less, wasn't a priority. He had decided to not say anything about it so he wouldn't create a scene in front of everyone and the cameras.

Later that night, despite his silent anger toward her, he didn't try to stop her advances as she climbed into bed next to him. She had a way with him, and he could never find a way to say no to her. But that particular night, every time he would kiss her or look into her eyes, he would see Larkin and be transported back to that night they shared together. He suddenly realized he didn't belong there with Abigail. He belonged with Larkin. He quickly put a stop to what they were doing, got dressed, and went downstairs to gather his thoughts. He grabbed his phone to call Larkin before Abigail came and interrupted him.

"Ryan, what's wrong?" Her tone was that of anger. Anger because he had stopped what they were doing.

"Abby, I can't do this anymore. I can't let you keep manipulating me into loving you. I thought I did love you, but I was wrong."

"How am I manipulating you, Ryan? I didn't force you to come here."

"No, you didn't, but you certainly know the right things to say, and the right things to wear, and the right looks to give me."

"Ryan, we belong together. You know we do."

"Why? Because we look good on each other's arm?"

"No, because we love each other."

"No, Abigail. This isn't love. You love the fame and the fortune that we give each other. You love the excitement of this industry. You love the physical relationship we share. But there is so much more to true love than just physicality."

"How would you know that? You act as if you've experienced true love before."

"I have. And regrettably, I left it behind when I came back here, and I don't know if I will be able to get it back."

"Who? Larkin? Come on, Ryan, that's not true love. You just feel sorry for her, that's all. She's the one manipulating you."

Ryan couldn't believe what had just come out of Abigail's mouth. "Are you kidding me, Abby? If Larkin were manipulating me then why would she have pushed me away? She's the one who encouraged me to come back to you."

Neither of them said anything for a while.

Finally, Ryan broke the silence. "Abigail, you are not a bad person. I just hope that one day you will be able to experience true love because there is nothing like it. You need to get *your* priorities straight and realize what is important in life. Because it is not this. Trust me."

The next morning, Ryan walked out of Abigail's life forever. He didn't know if Larkin would take him back, but he was going to do everything he could to fight for her. He landed that evening in Atlantic City and stopped by to check on the house he and Larkin had shared, as well as the boat. He made a phone call to someone he had been working with on a project before he had gone back to Los Angeles and then nervously drove his SUV across the bay to Larkin's parents' house. He couldn't stop the shaking in his hands as he pondered what he could possibly say to her.

Larkin's father hesitantly allowed Ryan into their home to see her. He could tell he wasn't happy with him. It wasn't too late, but she had already gone to bed.

"How is she, sir?"

"She's okay. Ryan, she's already been through enough with the cancer and then you leaving…"

"I am not here to hurt her, I can assure you," Ryan interrupted.

After studying him for a while, Larkin's father finally let him pass, the turn of his head guiding Ryan toward the direction of the stairway.

Ryan found Larkin sleeping peacefully in her bed with the TV on in the background. He turned it off and climbed into the bed next to her, lightly brushing his fingers on her cheek. Seeing her face again assured him he was doing the right thing; he was supposed to be with her. Her eyes struggled to open, but when he was finally able to see those blue eyes he had missed, he mouthed the word "hi" to her.

She was surprised to see him. "Ryan? What are you doing here?"

"I belong here. I should have never left. Come home with me, Larkin."

She was still trying to wake up. "What about Abigail?"

"I don't love Abigail. I thought I did, but the truth is I love you, and I want you to come home."

"I can't give you what she can, Ryan."

"No, you're wrong. She can't give me what *you* can, what you already have given me."

"What's that?"

"True love. A home. A best friend. A lullaby. I didn't realize all of this until you were no longer in my life. But I know now we belong together. So, come home with me, Larkin. Let's keep on living."

Letter #20 - April 11, 2012

Dearest Ryan,

You have come back to me. I guess that saying "if you love someone, set them free; if they come back it was meant to be" is true. I can't believe you have come back to me. Why are you so good to me?

We came back to our home yesterday, and we picked up right where we left off. We shared another amazing night together. It was what I needed to truly believe that you do love me and that you do want to be here with me. We are back in our old routine, and just like always, you left this morning for your daily fishing trip. I know how excited you were to get back on your boat.

I want to tell you about how worried I was about you earlier this afternoon. I awoke to a heavy fog and light drizzle, and I know you are smart enough to know better than to take the boat out in this weather, but you were not home and neither was the boat. I tried to call you twice, but you never answered; however, I am not surprised. I know there is never a good cell phone signal in the middle of the bay, but it was later than normal. You were usually back by then. I tried to focus on my manuscript, but my emotions were all over the place. I had just had an amazing night with the man of my dreams, your proposal from weeks ago was still on my mind (although neither of us have mentioned it), I was nervous about your safety, and of course, the leukemia is never far from my mind. My brain was bruised and battered from all the thoughts that were rushing in and out.

I paced from one room to the other. I prepared a pot of coffee. I unloaded the dishwasher. I folded yesterday's laundry and put a new load in. I swept the back deck, wiped down the patio furniture, and watered the newly planted spring bulbs that border the side of the house. I prepared a meatloaf and stored it in the fridge to be cooked later for our dinner. I read two chapters from the novel I had just started three nights ago. I vacuumed the carpets before transferring the laundry from the washer to the dryer. I felt like I had done a day's worth of chores, but only two hours had passed and still no sign of you.

I gathered my thoughts, grabbed my novel, and climbed under the covers of our king-sized bed. Before I knew it, my escape into the novel was interrupted by the sound of the boat engine as it pulled into the dock. I quickly rose to look out the window and saw you tying the rope from the boat to the cleat. I watched as you rinsed the boat off with the hose, locked up all the compartments, and finally, put the cover on the boat to protect it from the rain. I noticed you were carrying a small plastic bag and, of course, your daily bouquet of flowers you bring me every day. This time, red roses. You have no idea how happy I was to see you.

I waited by the sliding glass door as you greeted me with your crooked smile, making your way up the deck stairs. I craved your embrace.

"Hey! I was worried about you," I said, my craving satisfied as you wrapped me up in your arms. You didn't have the usual smell of saltwater, fish, and bait that you normally have when you get home.

"I didn't go very far. I know better," you assured me.

"How was fishing?"

"Actually, I didn't go fishing today. I went somewhere else. What did you do this morning?" you quickly asked as if you were trying to change the subject.

"I cleaned the house." I couldn't help but chuckle.

"Oh really? So I guess you are feeling pretty good today, huh?"

"Actually, yes," I agreed.

"Good, because I want to take you somewhere. You up for it?"

"I would love to. Where?"

"It's a surprise."

I love surprises, and I can't wait to see where you are taking me. I am writing this letter as I sit next to you in the SUV. But you keep wanting to hold my hand, so I am going to end this letter. I have a feeling I will want to write another one after this surprise you have for me. Until then.

Ryan closed the letter with a smile on his face. That was a great day with Larkin, and he remembered the night before as fondly as she had remembered it in the letter. And the surprise? That was pretty special, too. He closed his eyes reliving that moment.

Ryan loved feeling Larkin's hand wrapped in his as they rested on the center console.

"What are you writing over there?" he inquired.

"Nothing important," she said, trying to disregard his curiosity. He decided to leave her alone about it. She would share what she was working on with him when she was ready. He weaved his SUV in and out of traffic as if they were the only ones on the road. Thankfully, there wasn't too much traffic. Ocean City and the surrounding towns became ghost towns anytime it rained, and that day was no exception. His heart was pounding with anticipation of what was to come when they arrived at their destination. But for now, he was going to savor the ride with her. As they got closer, Ryan pulled over and put a blindfold over Larkin's eyes so she wouldn't be able to see the surprise once they got there.

When they arrived, he carefully guided her out of the SUV and into the driveway of a two-story five-bedroom house that sat along the inlet in Longport, New Jersey. He walked her to the back deck that extended to a private beach and dock that sat between two sand dunes just before the water met the earth. The deck gave way to a breathtaking view of Ocean City as it nestled under the Longport Bridge right across the inlet.

"Okay. Are you ready?"

"Yes!" He could tell she was anxious.

He took her blindfold off, and as she looked around and took in her surroundings, he couldn't help but wonder what she was thinking. He could tell she was having a hard time figuring out what to say.

"Ryan." She paused, looking around again at the house and the beach. "Ryan, where are we? Whose house is this?"

"Well, Larkin," he paused for a moment, "it's our house."

She quickly turned her head and fixated her eyes onto his. "What?"

"It's our house. I have had my eye on it for a while. Since before I left. I just bought it. That's where I was this morning. It will be our home after we get married." He could see the surprise on her face as he said those words. Ryan knelt down before Larkin, reached into his pocket, and pulled out a box that housed an engagement ring he had picked out for her earlier that morning. He grabbed her hand. "I meant what I said that first night we were together. I didn't forget what I said to you." He paused for a moment before he found the courage to say those words again. "Marry me, Larkin."

Her hand pulled quickly out of his, and she cupped her face with her hands, trying to hold back her emotions. He watched her as she shook her head no, repeating several times that she couldn't marry him. "Ryan, I can't marry you," she said with tears running down her cheeks.

"Larkin, why? Why can't you marry me?" His heart was trying to understand where she was coming from. He knew she loved him. Why wouldn't she marry him?

"Ryan, I love you, and I want to marry you more than anything, but you deserve a lifetime of love. I can't promise you a lifetime."

He stood up and pulled her hands away from her face and wiped her tears.

"No, but I can promise you yours."

CHAPTER 10

Letter #21 - April 28, 2012

My dearest Ryan,

We are tangled up together on the recliner next to the burning fireplace. I am sitting on your lap as you sleep, your arms wrapped around my waist. I am watching you as you dream, listening to you breathe. You have the most amazing face, you know that? I am resting my head on your chest, and your heartbeat is serenading me as I write this letter to you. We had the most amazing day today. Our wedding day. It couldn't have been more perfect. I felt like an angel in my sleek, white lace, spaghetti-strapped gown, and as I moved toward you down the aisle, all I could see was your crooked smile. I thought I was an angel walking down the aisle to heaven.

Thank you for an extraordinary day. Everything came together in such a short time. We had a small wedding, but I wouldn't have wanted it any other way. Our family and closest friends. My father giving me away to you. You and me together. Nothing is better.

We agreed to say our own vows, but I struggled because there are no words to describe how I feel for you and what you mean to me. I could feel you squeeze my hand as I struggled to find the right words to say. I stared down toward the ground, digging my toes into the cold, white sand. I studied the tiny grains of sand and gathered my thoughts, and the moment I looked up and saw your perfect face smiling at me, I knew exactly what I wanted to say. I don't ever want you to forget my words to you today. So here they are just in case.

"You wipe away my tears, you wipe away my sweat, you wipe away my blood, and you wipe away my sickness. You are my breath when I can't breathe. You are my warmth in the coldness. You are my light in the darkness. You are my heaven when I am going through hell. You are my voice when I lose mine. You are my sight when I am too tired to open my eyes. And you hold my eyes closed when I can't sleep. You never let me fall asleep alone. You are my smile when all I want to do is cry. You carry me when I can't walk. You pick me up when I fall, although it is rare that you even let me fall. You are my hero, my soldier, my angel, my hope. Every time you kiss me, you save me a little more each time. You have been my best friend since the beginning, and you will be until the end. You are my little piece of heaven, and I can only pray that I can be a little piece of yours. I love you more than

my life, and I vow to adore you the way you adore me."

I love you, my husband, always and forever.

Ryan and Larkin's wedding day was the best day of his life. He couldn't imagine a more perfect day, a more perfect time, and a more perfect girl. It had been the perfect April evening for a wedding. The sun had just started to sink behind the horizon, and the stars had just began to faintly appear one by one in the navy blue sky as guests filled the seats in the folded white chairs that sunk into the sand. They just moved into their new house, and they got married on the beach property that it sat on. It was a perfect sixty degrees, and the breeze that had been blowing all day had finally settled. It had only been two weeks since he had proposed, but it had been more than enough time to plan for the wedding. He had wanted to get married as quickly as possible. He didn't know what the future held for Larkin, and he wanted to be her husband for as long as he could. They had a makeshift altar prepared, and it sat just next to the dunes where Ryan and Larkin would go to feed the seagulls. The aisle was designated by a trail of red roses that led from the bottom of the deck steps all the way to the altar. They didn't have many guests, just immediate family and their closest friends—Larkin's parents and sister, Laura; her closest friends from school, Mary, Jennifer, and Nikki; his mother and two brothers, Ricky and Bobby, and their wives; and his closest friends, Ian, Sarah, and Justin. Ian had stood by Ryan as his best man, and Larkin had been attended to by Laura.

The tired sun had sunk like it was in quicksand, and by the time Larkin's figure had appeared at the end of the aisle with her father, it had transformed into the moon. The strums from violins echoed off the stars, preparing the guests for her arrival. As she had approached closer and closer, the moon lit up her face, and her angelic silhouette loomed through the candle lights that had been lit at the end of every chair aisle.

As he watched her walk down the sandy aisle arm-in-arm with her father, he realized he was meant to be her husband. She was more beautiful than any girl he had ever laid his eyes on. The white moonlight that gleamed down provided the only light in the darkness of the night, and as her silhouette materialized through the cloudiness of the light, all he could focus on were her beautiful ocean blue eyes. He was mesmerized by her beauty and by her strength, and he knew then he was meant to only ever love one woman, and that woman was about to become his wife.

How could he ever forget those vows that Larkin had said? After she had said them, for a brief moment, he had let go of her hand to wipe away the single tear streaming down her cheek. She then took the ring from her sister and placed it on his left ring finger. "Ryan, take this ring as a sign of my solemn vow." She sealed her vow with a kiss of the ring as it circled around his finger.

Ryan turned his head and stared at the ocean, watching the waves crash in. He was taken aback by the words she had spoken to him. After a moment, he looked into her eyes and began to speak. "Just like the ocean, my love for you is immense. I never knew what love was until you. I thought I did, but I was wrong. When I look at you, I see the strongest, most courageous woman. Even though it took a long time to get to this moment in our lives, I have loved you forever. It just took a tragedy to make me realize it." He paused. "And I am *so* sorry for that. I promise to fill your days making up for all the moments we have missed together. People ask me all the time how difficult it was for me to leave my career behind, and I don't even think twice about it when I answer them. I tell them it was the easiest decision I ever made. My mother used to say to me, 'Ryan, you were born to be an actor.' But just a couple of months ago, she said, 'Ryan, I was wrong. You weren't born to be an actor. You were born to take care of Larkin. I truly believe I brought you into this world to love and take care of that girl.' Larkin, I love you more than *my* life, and I vow to keep wiping away your tears, your sweat, your blood, and your sickness any time you need me to."

Ian placed Larkin's ring in Ryan's hand as he turned to him after his vows. "Larkin, take this ring as a sign of my solemn vow." And as Larkin did a moment ago, he sealed his vow with a kiss of the ring as it wrapped around her delicate finger.

Their love echoed off the cool night sand, and as everyone stood with applause and excitement when the minister announced them as husband and wife, Ryan escorted his bride down to where the earth met the ocean, and that was where they kissed for the first time as husband and wife.

Letter #22 - April 30, 2012

Hey, husband,

I can't believe I get to call you that. Today is the day. The first day of the next journey in my life, with or without cancer. We had an unforgettable weekend. We became husband and wife in front of our closest friends and family, and we all celebrated together throughout the weekend till we couldn't anymore. It was the best three days of my life, and I owe it all to you. Why are you so good to me? Cancer didn't even cross my mind this weekend. Not once. For once, I had no worries. Just joy and hope. I have never felt more alive, more healthy, and more vivacious than these past few days.

But now, back to today. Today we find out if the cancer is gone. We find out if all the hard work, the sacrifices, the time, the money, and the suffering has paid off. I must admit to you, Ryan, I am scared. Scared that it is still seething through my veins, poisoning my body. I am not prepared to hear that news. I have felt so amazing these past few days that it is hard to imagine I am still sick.

But if "cancer" is the word we hear later today, I will continue to fight and battle with everything that I am. With you by my side, I can do anything. You steady my hand, and you are my

*guardian when all is crumbling. I know you won't
let me fall.*

Letter #23 - May 1, 2012

Dear Ryan,

*"Tomorrow" has been a frightening word
for me lately. It's just a word, but it's an important
word. Tomorrow is not promised, and it is certainly
unknown. No one knows what tomorrow holds. You
can plan for it, but it is not guaranteed. Tomorrow
is taken for granted, and until your tomorrow is
threatened, you will always take it for granted.*

*You know those famous mottos "Live in the
moment" and "Live for today"? Well, we have
spent the past eight months trying to live in the
moment. Not dwelling on what we missed out on in
the past, and not worrying about the future. Just
what was then and now, making the most of every
minute of the day. You have a little routine every
morning when we wake up. You kiss my nose and
brush your thumb across my forehead, and you say
the same thing every time. You say, "Larkin, all I
ask is that you give me today so I can prove to you I
am your tomorrow."*

*Well, Ryan, my beautiful-faced boy, when I
awoke this morning, I turned to you, kissed your
nose and brushed my thumb across your forehead,
and said to you, "Ryan, not only will I give you
today, but I will give you all my tomorrows." And
for the first time in a long time, I feel like living for
tomorrow. I know, I know. As I wrote earlier,*

people take tomorrow for granted, and I am going to, just this one time, just today. And I promise, it will be the only time I will, but I want to skywrite it, Ryan. I want to shout it into the springtime air. I am cancer-free! Cancer-free! But you are still so worried. The doctor told us with the type of leukemia I had, my remission can relapse at any time. I still have to take medicines every day to try to avoid any chance of that, but tomorrow is looking a little less scary for me right now, and I can't wait to see what it has to offer me. I beat cancer, Ryan. I beat it. We beat it. What is more challenging, more taxing, than fighting cancer? I can't think of anything. So whatever challenge tomorrow has to offer, bring it on. I feel like I can take on anything.

Letter #24 - May 7, 2012

Hey, Fish,

We finished moving the last of our things into our new house on the bay this past week. Ian, Sarah, and Justin came to help, and so did Ricky and Bobby. It is still so surreal to me. Living with you in this spectacular home with this picturesque view of the inlet just like I had always dreamed. And you made it happen for me. I would never be here if it weren't for you. Why are you so good to me?

Hanging out with Ian, Sarah, and Justin this past week has been so great. You have really great friends, and now I am lucky to call them my friends. Especially Ian. He is so great, Ryan. We bonded months ago when he stayed with me those couple of days, but this past week, we really strengthened that bond. I have to be honest with you. After this past week, I feel a sense of calmness. I am at peace knowing you will be in good hands if my health were to decline again. You know how you always tell me you will never let me fall? Well, I know Ian, Sarah, and Justin will never let you fall.

I want you to remember this week. Remember the five of us tossing the Frisbee on the beach, grilling out every night, going for boat rides into the back bay. Remember the surprise birthday party you threw for me. I really was surprised, even though you think I wasn't. It was such a great week. Sarah and I would paint and decorate the house while the three of you would go fishing and try to catch our dinner for the night. Sarah and I had such great conversations about life and just about being women. We would blare the radio so loud and sing and dance around the house like we were in a band. The neighbors probably thought we were crazy! Sarah is so beautiful, talented, and full of life. She certainly adores you, and what makes her so beautiful is that she doesn't even realize it. Sometimes I wonder how you never fell in love with her.

Justin and I had a conversation the night before they all left. He thanked me for loving you. He had been worried about you. Did you know that? He was worried you weren't going to be able to bounce back from the backlash from the media about your divorce with Abigail. I told him he was underestimating your strength. He talked about the bond you and I share and how lucky we are to have started to build that bond when we were kids. He wished he and Amanda had that sort of bond. Our bond is bottomless, timeless, and effortless. We worked hard building this bond, and I am going to protect it and guard it with everything I have. And I am going to work even harder making sure it is never broken.

Letter #25 - May 21, 2012

Hey, beautiful,

I went fishing with you today for the first time since I went into remission. Actually, for the first time in years. The last time we went fishing was when you came home for your dad's funeral. Do you remember that? We stayed out on the water from dawn till dusk just fishing and talking. I knew you were hurting, and I wasn't going to leave until I knew you were going to be okay.

The weather was perfect today. Clear blue skies and calm waters. The smell of the salt water wafted off the swells, and the rocking of the boat from the passing boats' wake had transported me back into the past. I couldn't help but remember all the times we spent out on the water together, unknowingly building a love that has lasted a lifetime, literally.

As you fished, I read more of my manuscript to you. You would frequently look over at me and listen carefully to every word that read off my lips. And as I would look up at you between sentences, you would give me a quick wink underneath that furrowed brow of yours. I am almost finished with it. Now that I am feeling better, I will be able to spend more time on it.

I wish you could see the way I see you. Your body is magical. Behind those soft brown eyes is an extraordinary man, one of God's masterpieces. As I watched you move around on this boat, as I watched your muscles come alive with each cast or reel of the line, I was watching a perfect piece of art come alive before my very eyes. I ask you so often why you are so good to me. But today, I am going to ask God why He is so good to me. For sending me you, He has been good to me, and I will never understand why I have been so lucky to have received such a perfect gift.

Letter #26 - June 4, 2012

My dearest Ryan,

As you know, one of my favorite things to do as a kid was to go to the drive-in movies. There was just something about watching a movie on a giant screen sitting inside the car eating popcorn and sipping on an Icee. My most favorite times were when Ricky would let you borrow the truck and we would go pick up Mary, Jennifer, and Nikki and whoever they were dating at the time; and your old friends, Scotty and Mike would come in Scotty's truck, and we would make the ten mile drive to the Absecon Drive-In Movie Theater. Do you remember that? It was our little circle of friends. Nothing was better than sitting in the back of that '89 Chevy pick-up truck on that navy blue fleece blanket with a cooler of sodas and candy, feeling the breeze coming off of the Absecon Bay. You and I always sat next to each other with our backs propped against the back window of the truck cab, and you would always let me use your shoulder as my pillow because I could never stay awake long enough to watch the entire double feature. I remember you would get so frustrated with me when I would ask you on the way home how the movie ended. "If you were that interested in the ending, you would have stayed awake," you would say to me, shaking your head.

One particular night at the drive-in I will never forget is when we went to see the double feature of "True Lies" and "The Mask" in the summer of 1994. The summer before my senior year. The summer after you graduated. I knew something was bothering you because you didn't want anyone else to come with us. It was just you and me. You didn't really say much to me throughout the night until the intermission.

That was the night you told me you were moving to Los Angeles to pursue your dream of being an actor. I'll never forget the feeling when I heard the words "I'm moving to LA, Larkin." As I listened to you talk about how excited you were about this epic change you were about to take in your life, your words started to morph into mumbles, and then eventually, I couldn't even hear anything you were saying as echoes of sorrow and anguish resonated inside my ears and my head. My heart dropped into my stomach, and my throat swelled up as if I was having an allergic reaction. I didn't say anything. I couldn't say anything. I was so devastated to lose my best friend. To this day, Ryan, I still don't know how I held back my tears. I never let you see me cry.

Unfortunately, drive-in movie theaters are pretty much nonexistent these days. It's a shame, really. I feel sorry for all the kids out there who won't get to experience those fun-filled nights with close friends hanging out in the back of a pick-up watching movies and forming bonds like we did. There's nothing like the drive-in movie theater.

Last night, after dinner, you asked me to go on a date with you. Of course, I accepted, and you wouldn't give me any hints as to where you were going to take me. When we got into the SUV, you blindfolded me so I couldn't see anything. I know you had to have been just a little bit annoyed with me because I kept asking you over and over again where you were taking me. You probably wished you had also put a gag in my mouth to shut me up!

You made one quick stop before you parked the SUV in a vacant parking lot overlooking the bay, and all I could hear was you fumbling around with something. I then heard you leave the front seat and get something from the back. My curiosity began to heighten after you came back and guided me out of the passenger seat and into the back seat of the SUV. You walked back around to the driver's side, and you climbed in next to me taking my blindfold off. And right before my eyes was our laptop set up on a box you had placed between the two front seats with "When Harry Met Sally" playing in the DVD drive. My all-time favorite movie! The movie we watched countless times together. You handed me a bag of popcorn and an Icee, and we watched the movie together with my head on your shoulder the entire time. But I didn't fall asleep. Not this time.

You are amazing, Ryan. You created our own little makeshift drive-in movie theater. You created another amazing memory for me to cherish, for you to cherish, too. Hopefully, you will keep making these memories, Ryan, because you may need them one day to help get you through the pain and sorrow. Know that these moments shared with you have helped to complete my life, and I want you to know you have made me the happiest that I could possibly be. Why are you so good to me?

Letter #27 - July 5, 2012

Dear Ryan,

Another great night last night. Ian and Linda, Sarah, and Justin and Amanda came to visit us for the Fourth of July holiday, and the seven of us spent the night in our pitched tent on the beach behind the house. We were in our own little world playing two-hand touch football and dancing and laughing as the fireworks lit up the black, endless sky. We had tiki lamps set up with a big bonfire, and we roasted hot dogs and marshmallows with songs from the likes of Norah Jones and Frank Sinatra in the background serenading the sultry summer air. We were on our own private island. An island where sickness and pain doesn't exist. Only strength, love, and friendship. An island where the seven of us play endless games of two-hand touch football and dance underneath the fireworks.

Several times last night, I found myself imagining we were in heaven and nothing could touch us. I often wonder what heaven is really like. I can't imagine it is any better than when I am with you. I imagine it with endless beaches surrounded by crystal clear blue waters and eternal sunshine and warmth. I imagine a place where sleep is nonexistent and love bears all. Heaven is our own private island. It's ironic, don't you think? For many people, heaven is a real, unimaginary place, but no one knows what it really, truly is like. All you can do is imagine what it could be like. All I know is I can't imagine it without you.

Letter #28 - August 1, 2012

Hey, lovely,

This summer has been extraordinary. I'm healthy. We're happy and in love, and there is no better way to bring the summer to an end than you going back to work. This has what I have been hoping for. You have sacrificed so much for me. You put your life on hold, and now it is time to get back to it. You're not going to be too far away. Atlanta. Not so bad. At least it is the same country this time.

I started to write to you when I found out I was sick. Well, I am not sick anymore, but I decided I am still going to write to you anyway. I don't know when I will stop or when I will give these letters to you, but I imagine I will know when the time comes.

The summer of 2012 is one I will never forget. Married in our new home on the bay. Just like I had always dreamed of, and you made my dreams come true. I still don't have that yacht I always wanted, but your Grady White is certainly not too shabby of a boat. Fishing, grilling, Jet Skiing, dancing, walking hand-in-hand on the beach with the water up to our ankles, enjoying frequent visits with Ian and Linda, Justin and Amanda, and Sarah, feeding the seagulls at the dunes, watching the boats go by as we sit tangled together on our beach in front of the bonfire, making love as the rain pounds against the bedroom's French door windows. A summer to remember. And hopefully, an illness to forget.

We leave tomorrow for Atlanta. I am so excited to see you get back to work. To see you in your element. I'm going to miss Jersey, but we'll be back before we know it.

CHAPTER 11

The steaming, hot water from the shower was becoming lukewarm as the droplets streamed down Ryan's tired body. He was able to get a few hours of sleep in between the twenty-some letters he had read with an occasional dream about Larkin. He could never really tell if he was actually dreaming or if she really had been there with him. She felt real, and her smell was almost tangible.

As he towel-dried off, he was startled by the sudden music that had started to resonate throughout the house. It was fitting, really. Their song. Their wedding song. "Nice 'n' Easy". He had installed a surround-sound system in the house for Larkin because she loved to listen to music when she would write or clean the house. But something was wrong with the stereo because it would just randomly turn on every so often. Larkin had left her "Frank Sinatra Greatest Hits" CD in the drive, and he didn't have it in him to change it. He actually enjoyed it when it would start to play, and he would listen to the entire CD before he turned it off. It reminded him of her.

He finished dressing into a loose pair of gray sweatpants and a black T-shirt, and as he exited the bathroom, he saw her. She was standing there before him holding a white cyclamen out for him to take. Her favorite flower.

"I got your flowers. They're beautiful." She slowly walked toward him. "Dance with me?"

He took the flower from her hand and wrapped his left arm around her waist and took her left hand into his other hand and rested it on his chest.

"You're beautiful," he whispered in her ear, and their bodies moved as one to the music. He pulled her close, capturing her scent. They danced close for a while before he pulled away to look into her eyes.

"I miss you, Larkin. I miss you so much."

She smiled at him. He loved when she smiled at him. She ran her fingers through his hair.

"You're beautiful, Ryan. My beautiful-faced boy."

"Larkin." He paused, struggling to push the words through his mouth. "Larkin, I am so sorry. I am so sorry I wasn't there with you. I promised you I would be there with you, and I wasn't. I left you all alone."

She stopped their bodies from swaying and pulled his face into her hands.

"You were there, baby. Don't you

remember? You were there. You were waiting for me. You were standing there with a bouquet of cyclamens. And you embraced me, and you told me you loved me. You wouldn't let go of me, and I told you it was okay. Don't you remember? You need to remember."

"I remember wanting to stay with you. I didn't want to leave you. I should have stayed with you, Larkin."

"No, you shouldn't have." She wiped the tears from his face. "No, I didn't want you to stay. You promised me you were going to keep on living. That's the promise you need to keep."

He pulled her close to him again and savored every touch, every breath, and every heartbeat as they danced together. He could feel her breath as she whispered she loved him in his ear.

And then she was gone.

Ryan looked over at the clock. It was 8:00 a.m. He felt like time had been standing still for the past two months. He never left the house. An occasional trip to the store was the only thing that would ever really pull him away. He felt that if he left the house, he was leaving her. He could still feel her presence inside the house. Her presence was so real to him. Every room he walked into, he could see her. In the living room, he would see her typing on her laptop as she sat on the couch in front of the fireplace. In the kitchen, he would see her preparing their dinner. In the dining room, he would see her preparing a vase for the fresh flowers he had brought to her that morning. In the bedroom, he would see her drying off just after a shower. Her ghost was everywhere, and he was afraid of the day it would no longer be there. He was afraid to move on because she would stop coming to him. And he wasn't ready yet. He didn't know if he ever would be.

The storm had passed, and it was an unusually warm morning for late March. Signs of springtime were ascending upon the Jersey Shore, and the letters had unburied memories of fishing and boating. It was the perfect weather for a boat ride, he thought. He hadn't been back on the water since last summer, the last time being with her. He sat on the edge of the bed as the music continued to fill the empty, melancholy air, and he thought about the encounter he just had with Larkin. He *had* made her a promise that night, the last night he was with her. And he wasn't keeping it. He had already broken one promise to her, and he needed to find the strength to keep this one. He grabbed the rest of the unread letters off the nightstand, grabbed his sweatshirt, and headed downstairs to grab the boat keys from the garage. He needed to at least try. Try to ready himself to move on. That way, he could tell her that he was trying the next time she came to him. If there was a next time. It scared him to think there might not be.

He motored his *Grady White* along the medium-sized swells of the inlet through the Great Egg Harbor Bay into the back bays of Ocean City. He found a spot where no one else was close and let the boat drift in stride with the current while he continued to read her letters.

Letter #29 - September 10, 2012

Hey, beautiful-faced boy,

Leukemia is no laughing matter. It is terrifying, it's daunting, it's forbidding, and it's intimidating. It is sinister, it's devilish, it's hostile, and it's unforgiving. It is everything that laughter is not. Leukemia is a sharp knife that severs life. And you, Ryan, always do everything you can to help dull that knife. Cancer is a strange and unpredictable cell. You can go for years in remission, and then one day it pops its head up again. If you ever have it, you will never be free of it.

We just got home from the hospital. Four days of IVs, dull hospital food, and nothing to look at but four white walls and nurses and doctors in and out of the room all day. It's funny. I hate hospitals. I'm a nurse, and I hate hospitals.

You never left my side. You fought tooth and nail to be able to lay in the bed with me, and of course, you won. You're Ryan Boone. Everything comes easy to you, remember? I'm just kidding. I actually think the one nurse, Julia, had a crush on you. She would have let you do anything.

I don't remember anything. The last thing I remember is walking into the kitchen to pour myself a glass of milk, and the next thing I remember is waking up in the hospital. I haven't been feeling well the past several weeks, and we thought it was just a bad cold. We had left for Atlanta so you could start filming the movie you had postponed when I was getting treatment. I finally was well enough for you to feel comfortable going back to work. I went with you the first two weeks, but I came home to see the doctor after I came down with a cold. I started to feel better after a couple of days, but I decided to stay home for another week to spend time with my parents and Laura since she came home for a few days to visit.

Shortly after, my cold came back and was actually worse. I was running a low-grade fever with night sweats, and I had no appetite. You were worried, as always, and made arrangements to come home, but you couldn't for a couple of days, so you asked Ian to come stay with me for a few days until you could come. Thankfully, he is in New York so he was close by. I begged you not to call him, but you insisted, and like I said earlier, you're Ryan Boone and you always win! Well, it also helps that I have a crush on you, too, just like Nurse Julia.

I guess you were right, though. Thank God Ian was there. Thank God because who knows how long I would've laid on the kitchen floor until someone found me. I woke up in the hospital with you lying next to me. My parents, Laura, and Ian were by my side, too. I remember feeling very scared because everybody had such a look of worry on their faces. Everybody but you. You, of course, had that crooked smile that is so amazing. It made me feel less worried to see you smiling at me.

We visited for about an hour with everyone before they left. I was so tired, and I was having abdominal pain, and my head hurt but I didn't know why. I said something to you about it, and you told me you needed to tell me something. You were lying next to me on your side, and you shifted your upper body up onto your elbow, raising you up so I could see your face better. You brushed my cheek and my forehead, and as I looked into your eyes, that crooked smile faded away. My heart sank into my stomach, and the tears that were building up in your eyes were enough to send chills down my spine.

You explained everything to me. How Ian found me on the kitchen floor and rushed me to the hospital. How he called you right away, and you came as fast as you could. How they had to remove my spleen because it was enlarged, and they had to put three stitches above my left eyebrow because I had hit my head when I fell. You explained that I was hooked up to IV antibiotics because I developed pneumonia. I was dehydrated, and that was why I fainted in the kitchen. My immune system wasn't able to fight off my cold, and that alarmed the doctors because it should have been able to if I was in remission. My enlarged spleen and lymph nodes were also bad signs, so the doctors did some blood tests and a lymph node biopsy.

I remember when I first started writing to you. I had just found out that I had leukemia, and I hadn't told you yet. It took me months to be able to tell you. And I am still writing to you. Eighteen

months later. And this time, you're telling me.
You're telling me I am sick again. But it's worse,
Ryan. It is much worse than eighteen months ago.
What are we going to do?

Ryan thought back on that day in the hospital when he had explained to Larkin that she had acquired a very rare complication that can arise with her type of leukemia called Richter's Syndrome. It can appear suddenly, even in patients that are in remission. The prognosis is generally poor. She had been assigned to the high-risk category based on her test results, which meant they didn't feel she would respond positively to the treatment. Telling her that she was very sick and that she may only have several months left to live was the hardest day of his life. Even harder than when he found out she had leukemia. He had felt empty inside. He stayed every night with her in the hospital, and when she was sleeping, he would climb out of bed and close himself in the bathroom and cry harder than he had ever cried before. He never wanted her to see him cry. There was no way he could lose her. She had beaten the cancer. She had been happy, energetic, and vibrant again. Just like when they were kids. How could this have happened? These were all the things that had flooded his mind when he had found out she was dying. He had felt like he was dying.

As the weeks passed by, Larkin's condition had remained stable. She was getting weekly IV antibiotic treatments to try to slow down the progression of the Richter's Syndrome. Ryan didn't return to work and had to put production of the movie on hold. They spent every waking moment together, and he never left her side except for half an hour every morning when she was still sleeping. He would walk to the corner of the main road to Harry's Flower Shop to buy her a fresh bouquet of flowers, just like he had been doing every day since he moved back with her.

Some days she felt strong enough for them to take a walk on the beach or to go out to dinner. But it wasn't often. They spent their days watching movies, playing cards and board games, visiting with her parents, Laura, his mother, Ricky and Bobby; and Ian, Sarah, and Justin would make frequent visits, too. She sometimes would try to write, but he could tell she had lost the motivation to finish. She would sit in front of the laptop for about thirty minutes before she would shut it and go upstairs and lie down. She was changing right before his eyes. The Larkin who was his childhood best friend, the Larkin who he was so madly in love with, was losing strength and courage. Her optimism was quickly fading, and he could tell she was becoming depressed. He did everything he could to make her smile and laugh.

Letter #30 - October 5, 2012

My beautiful husband,
I am sitting on the deck as you sleep not too

far away inside on the couch in front of the burning fireplace. It is late, and the moon is heavy like my heart. This may very well be my last letter to you. I don't know. I don't know how much longer I have with you. I have been feeling sorry for myself these last couple of weeks. It's pretty pathetic. I have never been one to feel sorry for myself, but I do, and I can't help it. I need to write my feelings down because I can't say them to you because I know I will cry. And I don't want you to see me cry anymore.

There are too many things I haven't done yet. Too many sunsets and sunrises I haven't seen. Too many dances I haven't danced. Too many songs I haven't sung. Too many books I haven't read. Too many books I haven't written. Too many miles I haven't traveled. Too many "I love you's" I haven't said. Too many hugs I haven't given. Too many tears I haven't cried. Too many laughs I haven't laughed. Too much love that I haven't been able to give.

Love is home. Love is laughter. Love is an embrace. Love is the foundation of our soul. Love is the engine that keeps us motoring through life's journey. You're my love, and you have given me reason to motor on through life as long as I have been able to this past year.

I thought we were in the clear, that I had beaten this unrelenting enemy. But I was wrong. But I want you to know that I have finally made peace with the fact that I am going to die. I am going to die very soon. I now need you to find peace with it. I

*hear you get out of bed every night and lock
yourself in the bathroom. I hear you crying. Ever
since that night when you came to see me, when you
confronted me about being sick, I have never seen
you cry. You are too good to me to ever let me see
you cry. Why are you so good to me?*

*With each letter I continue to write, I fear it
will be my last. So unlike my previous twenty- nine
letters, I am going to end each one by telling you I
love you.*

I love you, Ryan.

Ryan will never forget the night he forgot to
lock the bathroom door. Larkin had had a bad day,
and he was upset with the suffering she had to
endure. The weekly IV antibiotics were making her
sick for days, and she maybe had two good days out
of every week. It was starting to eat at him. He was
having a hard time keeping control.

Larkin had been sick most of the day, and
she didn't know it, but while he held her tight as she
cried herself to sleep, he was crying, too. It was
2:30 a.m., and she finally fell asleep. Or at least he
thought she had. He, as quietly as he could, slipped
out of bed and went into the bathroom to splash
some cold water on his face. As he looked at
himself in the mirror, he could see himself falling
apart. His red and swollen eyes, his week-old beard
clinging to his face, his trembling hands as he wiped
his face dry with a towel. He was not this strong
man that Larkin thought of him to be. As fear and

sorrow took over his body, his legs weakened, and he fell to the cold, marble-tiled floor and began to sob. He finally had lost all control of his emotions, and her impending death that once seemed impossible to him was now becoming a reality.

As he tried to gain control of his emotions so he could return back to the bed to be with Larkin, he felt her soft, frail hands grab his head as it rested on his knees, and he looked up at her as she cradled his face in her hands.

"Kiss me, Ryan. Anytime you feel like crying, you kiss me, okay?" She pressed her lips against his and held them there for a while before slowly pulling them away. "It's okay to cry, Ryan." She sat next to him and rested the side of her head against his while she grabbed his hand and interlaced her fingers with his.

"It's okay to cry. Crying isn't a sign of weakness, Ryan. It's a sign of strength. It's the weakness leaving your body so you can have the strength you need to get through this." She stroked the side of his head as it fell onto her shoulder. "Why do you think I cry so much?"

"I don't want you to die, Larkin. I need you to live. I don't think I can live without you."

"It's going to be okay. You're going to be okay." She rested her cheek on his head as they sat there for a long while without saying anything. She just continued to caress the side of his head with her fingers and telling him everything was going to be okay.

After calmness finally released the grip that the fear and sorrow had had on his body, he lifted her up off the floor and carried her back to the bed and let her fall asleep in his arms; this time, he reassured her that everything was going to be okay.

Letter #31 - October 13, 2012

Happy birthday, dear Ryan,

Ian, Sarah, and Justin came to help me throw you a birthday party. I think it went well, don't you? I wanted it to be a surprise, but it's pretty hard to plan a surprise party when you are by my side every minute of the day. But I don't mind. I like having you by my side. I can feel my body weakening, but I am trying hard to be strong. I am trying hard to not let you see me struggle.

We had an intimate party, just you and me, Ian and Linda, Sarah, Justin and Amanda, Joan and Russell, Laura, your mom, Ricky and Jill, and Bobby and Jane, and even Lou from next door made an appearance. I made sure Ian brought you the biggest cake he could find, and I loaded it up with thirty-six candles. It was so big, Ian and I had to carry it to you together. You never took your eyes off me as we all sang "Happy Birthday" to you. Everyone brought you amazing gifts, and you seemed to be having a good time. Everyone seemed to be having a good time. Laughing, smiling, and catching up. It was so nice to see everyone like that. I can't have a conversation with my mother anymore without her bursting into tears. I hope you had a good time, Ryan. It is tradition to make a wish as you blow out the candles. But as you blew out the candles tonight, I made a wish for you. My wish for you, Ryan, is to have many more good times. Life is too short to not.

Happy birthday, Ryan. Make a wish. I love you.

His birthday party was when he realized just how sick Larkin was becoming. She was still strong, but her body became tired faster than it had ever before. He could see how much she struggled to stand when she and Ian held the cake as everyone sang to him. He could see Ian's arm around her waist holding her upright. She was tired from the day's activities, and she was right when she said she did everything she could to not let him see her struggle. She did everything she could to keep a smile on her face as she stood there waiting for him to blow out the candles. And she was also right about all the amazing gifts that everyone had brought, especially hers. She had put together a photo album of pictures starting from their childhood all the way up to the present. It was the best gift he had received all night. She gave it to him in private, after he realized she had retired upstairs without telling him. She had asked Ian to help her upstairs because she wanted to lie down, but she didn't want him to know because she didn't want to interrupt the good time he was having with his family and friends. But he did notice. And Ian had told him where she was.

"Hey! You okay, baby?" he asked as he climbed into the bed next to her.

"Yes, I just wanted to lie down for a moment. I'm okay. Go back downstairs to your party."

"I will. I just wanted to check on you."

"Hey, open the nightstand drawer. I have a present for you."

"You do? Larkin, you didn't have to get me a gift. Every minute I get to spend with you is a gift."

"I made it. I want you to have it."

Ryan pulled a photo album out of the drawer, and they looked at it together, reminiscing about all the memories that each picture symbolized. When they got to the last page, Ryan noticed several blank pages.

"Ryan?" she whispered.

"Yeah?"

"I don't want to die in a hospital. I want to die in your arms with no one else around. Not my parents, not our friends. Just you. I want everyone to be happy, like they are downstairs. I don't want them crying over me. I can't handle it. I just want peace. I just want you."

"Are you sure, Larkin? I don't know if your parents are going to be okay with that."

"I'll talk to them. They'll give me what I want. What makes me happy."

"Okay. If that's what you want, then I will make sure it happens. I promise you that you won't die alone, that you'll die in my arms, okay?" He kissed the top of her head as he felt his chest get heavy.

"And, Ryan, I don't want to spend my last days or months or whatever I have left just sitting around playing card games and watching movies. I want to travel and see things I have never seen. I am feeling strong enough right now to do this. I want to do this before I can't. I left those pages in the album blank so we can fill them with new memories when we travel."

Ryan didn't know what to say. He was worried that traveling would take its toll on her body and that it would accelerate her death. But she had begged and pleaded with him that it was what she wanted, and at that point, there was nothing he wouldn't do for her. He would go hungry, he would walk on water, he would hold her for a thousand years, and he would carry her to the ends of the earth if that was where she wanted to go.

CHAPTER 12

Letter #32 - December 25, 2012

Dearest Ryan,

Merry Christmas, my love. These past two months have been like living in a dream. You have taken me to see unbelievable places, and we have taken adventures that I never thought I would have ever taken, even if I was healthy. You have more than kept your promise to me about making the last days of my life miraculous. You have over exceeded. We've been to Hawaii, Australia, Paris, Rio de Janeiro, and Mexico. We have been so busy that I haven't really had any time to write to you. But I am making the time now. I need you to remember the day you gave me yesterday. It was by far the best day of these last two months together, and that is saying a lot because these last two months have been a perfect ending to what I think has been a perfect life...

For the length of Larkin's sickness, Ryan had always believed she would pull through and beat this disease. He never thought twice about it. But during those last few weeks of her life, as he saw her slowly slipping away from week to week, he knew he was going to lose her. The last two months of Larkin's life, although difficult at times, were ironically the best times of Ryan's life. He was amazed at how strong and positive she was even in the face of death. She wanted to live the rest of her life to the fullest, and he made sure she did. For two months, they traveled the world together doing things he never thought he would do. She had requested that she spend what little time she had left with Ryan. She said her good-byes to her family and closest friends before they left, much to their and Ryan's disapproval, but they obliged because it was what she wanted. Larkin did not want anyone fussing over her, and she couldn't bear to see her parents grieving over her. She felt that this would be in the best interest of not only her parents but her as well. Seeing them suffer over her dying was too stressful for her, and she wanted her last months to be peaceful. And Ryan was her peace.

She chose to stop the weekly IV antibiotic treatments because she was tired of being sick all the time. She instead started on a daily oral medicine with less side effects, but it also came with a decreased chance of prolonged life as compared to the IV drug. She felt as if that was a sacrifice worth taking. At least she would enjoy the last days of her life. It was mid-October, and they started in Hawaii. He had arranged for them to stay in a private cottage in Maui, and they awoke every morning to symphonic birdsong and invigorating aromas of the air and blooming tropical flowers. The days Larkin felt strong, Ryan would take her on a new adventure. They went on a two-mile tandem ziplining trek that had given them a better vantage point of Maui than a flying eagle. They swam with dolphins and manta rays, they went on helicopter and glass bottom boat tours, they went swimming underneath waterfalls, and they went horseback riding along the white, sandy beaches. The days that Larkin needed to rest, Ryan would lie holding her in the hammock that hung from two palm trees that shaded their private hut. They would lie for hours, and if she was able to stay awake, she would read to him. And every night, they would dance together. They would dance under the bright white moon as the soft grains of sand would caress their bare feet. Ryan would spin Larkin as they listened to the waves crash against the earth at the foot of their private sanctuary. They didn't need music. Their love was their music, and after each spin, Ryan would pull Larkin back in close to him, kissing her cheek, kissing her forehead, kissing her lips, followed by whispers of "I love you" in her ear.

Australia greeted Ryan and Larkin in the beginning days of November, and it was there where they dove the Great Barrier Reef, went white-water rafting, kayaked in the Coral Sea, and she held his hand as he sacrificed his fear of heights on the ultimate altar of Cairns Bungy Tower.

Ryan and Larkin ended November in Paris where they strolled hand-in-hand along the Seine, soaked up the city life from sidewalk cafes, relaxed at the Luxembourg Gardens, prayed at the Notre Dame Cathedral, and kissed under the Eiffel Tower.

And after spending most of December visiting the Harbor of Rio de Janeiro in Brazil and exploring the beaches of Cabo San Lucas in Mexico, Ryan could see Larkin slowly weakening, slowly succumbing to the strangling grasp of the cancer. He was losing her, and he was trying desperately to find any way to prolong her life.

He knew exactly what day she was going to write about in the letter. He had taken her back to the private cottage they shared in Hawaii, and it was there where he wanted to show her just how much he loved her, just how much she meant to him, and just how much these past twelve months had changed his life.

Ryan continued to read the letter.

...Yesterday was Christmas Eve, and the sun had warmed our small corner of the earth to a perfect seventy degrees. As I slept in, you held true to the daily tradition of bringing me flowers, pacing the grounds around the hut, gathering a bouquet of white gardenias, yellow plumeria, white and pink orchids, and white Hawaiian jasmine to present to me. You took one of the gardenias and gently stroked my face to wake me. I slowly opened my eyes, and I looked up at your beautiful face and swept the side of it with my hand.

"Hi, beautiful-faced boy," I greeted you. "Hi," you mouthed back. "How are you this morning?

"Any moment with you is extraordinary." I couldn't help but smile.

"Do you feel strong? I have something I want to do with you today."

As I sat up, you presented me with the hand-made bouquet you had just created, and I accepted it, bringing it to my nose, slowly inhaling, capturing the scent of the islands that emanated off the blooms. "I feel okay. What do you want to do?" I inquired. I knew you could tell I wasn't being completely honest.

"Well, I want you to take a long bath, and then put your favorite dress on and meet me outside by the veranda in one hour. I'll just be outside on the porch. I'm not far. Just yell if you need me, okay?" I nodded my head, and you kissed me before you left the room. I couldn't wait to see what you had in store for us.

After I finished putting my favorite dress on—a pale yellow sundress with lace straps that rested just below my knees—I made my way to the front of the cottage where I saw the bouquet of flowers you had made me that morning resting on the chair that sat next to the front door. A small piece of paper with the words "Bring these with you, and follow the roses" rested on top of the flowers. I grabbed the bouquet and nervously exited the cottage, wondering what it was you had planned. I had to be careful as my knees felt weak, like they could buckle at any given moment. I had to keep one hand outstretched against the wall or hold onto a piece of furniture. As I pushed the screened door open, I couldn't believe what my eyes were seeing. I stepped onto a rose petal–covered porch, and the petals extended down the porch steps onto the perfectly manicured lawn and ended at the foot of the veranda where I saw you standing inside, clothed in khaki dress slacks with a white button-down shirt, waiting for me as you stood in front of a priest. I knew at that moment what it was that you, my amazing man, had planned for us, and I did everything I could to hold back my emotions. I brought my hand up to my face as my eyes filled up with tears that represented every emotion you have brought to me this past year.

You approached me as I stood on the top step of the porch, and you reached out your hand to help me down, and after I reached your level, you knelt down on one knee and proposed to me. "Larkin, marry me again. Renew our vows with me. Let me prove to you just how much I love you."

I looked down at you, down into your brown eyes, and I gave you a nod, and with that, you stood up and picked me up and carried me to the makeshift altar on the veranda. As we stood face-to-face listening to the priest recite passages from the Bible, I held on to your hands as hard as I could, desperately trying not to fall to your feet. You pulled me in close and wrapped your arms around my waist so I didn't have to try so hard to stand. The priest offered the chance for us to say our vows.

"Larkin, I will continue to breathe so you can breathe. I will continue to stand so you can stand. I will continue to honor and love you as my

wife. You will never be alone. You will never be without me. I will be holding your hand till the very end." And just like our wedding day last April, you sealed your vow with a kiss on my ring that has never been removed from my finger.

"Ryan, you never cease to amaze me. You have changed my life in ways you can't begin to imagine. You have shown me the true meaning of life and love. You have made my life worth living. There is no better person than you, and I am happy just to have known you, and I am honored you let me love you." And as I also did on our wedding day in April, I sealed my vow with a kiss on your ring.

Thank you, Ryan. Thank you for an amazing day. Thank you for an amazing life. We may not have been together for all of it, but you have always been in my heart. Why are you so good to me?

I love you.

He remembered it just like she described it. After the priest had confirmed the renewal of their vows, he carried Larkin through the veranda, up the porch steps, and inside the cottage. He knew she was beginning to suffer, and it was killing him to see her that way. She was so weak and so tired all the time. He held her in his arms as they lay on the couch in front of the fire while he waited for the dinner he had ordered to be delivered. She was especially beautiful that day. The cancer may have taken her health and her strength, but it certainly hadn't taken away her beauty.

That night, Larkin had taken a turn for the worst. She ate very little at dinner, and she had come down with a low-grade fever and night sweats. She had vomited a couple of times but very little since she had nothing in her stomach. Ryan was scared. He was more scared that night than any other night he had been with her when she was sick. He stayed in bed with her and just held her as close as he could. He feared the worst.

"Larkin?" He paused for a moment. This had been the question he had been dreading. "Larkin? Tell me what you want. Tell me where you want to die." She didn't respond. He waited a moment to see if she would say anything. He knew she was awake. He could feel her breathing, and by then, he was able to tell if she was asleep or awake by the way she breathed. "Larkin? Please tell me what you want. Please tell me where you want to die."

She looked up at him for a moment, then returned her head to his chest.

"Home," she whispered. "I want to die in the house we made our home. I want to go home."

"Okay." He kissed the top of her head. "Okay. We'll go home."

"Ryan? I need you to do something for me."

"Anything, Larkin."

"I need you to call Ian and Sarah and Justin and make sure they are there when I die. Not in the room with us, but there at home. I want you to have

Justin make all the calls to our family and friends because he is good at things like that. He has a way of making people feel at ease." Ryan didn't say anything. He just listened.

"Are you listening to me, Ryan?" she asked sternly.

"Yes, of course I am."

"And I want Ian to carry me to the hearse after I am gone."

"What? No, Larkin. No. Why? Why Ian?" Ryan was angered by her strange request.

"Trust me, Ryan. You have to trust me. I want Ian to carry me to the hearse. Okay? You promise me this, okay?"

"Okay. I promise," he answered, holding back his tears. "And what about Sarah? What do you want Sarah there for?"

"To hold your hand, because you are going to need her."

Ryan could no longer hold his tears back, and as he began to cry, Larkin raised her head up and kissed him. "Remember, Ryan, anytime you want to cry, you kiss me."

Letter #33 - December 26, 2012

To my beautiful-faced boy.

We are journeying back home—home for me

to die. I had a bad night last night, and I know it scared you. I could see it in your eyes. Today was better. At least I feel strong enough to travel. You have been holding on to me as we sit on the airplane, and I actually pretended to fall asleep so you would, too, just so I could write this. I wanted to get one last letter in to you. Mainly because I know that you are wondering why I requested that Ian carry me to the hearse after I die. It's not because I don't want you to. It's because I don't want your last memory of me to be lying on a gurney. I want our last memory to be of us lying together with you holding me as my life ends.

One thing I learned from you was that whenever you do something you are afraid to do, regardless of the outcome, it is a victory. Fear is one's worst enemy, and you need to do everything in your power to not succumb to it. Fear keeps us from living. If you let fear prevail, then you might as well be dead. But how do you not give in to fear? Courage. And you, Ryan, are the most courageous person I know. Don't start letting fear overcome you now. You will need that courage now more than ever. Find a way to hold onto it, and don't ever let it go. You showed me how to find mine. Every smile, every laugh, every touch, every word, and every step you helped me take, and every breath you helped me breathe all gave me courage. And this letter symbolizes that courage. Keep it with you always, and you will never be without it.

I can only hope that you fully understand how grateful and indebted I will always feel to you for everything you have sacrificed for me. I don't know if it is possible to find the words to explain to you all that you have been to me, but let me at least try.

Love is too small of a word to describe how I feel for you. I love you so much, I can't breathe. You caught my heart as it fell for you, and you protected it, you nurtured it, and you honored it. The love I feel for you is majestic and angelic. It is timeless and breathless. It is miraculous and unqualified. It is unexpected, and it is unwavering. It leaves me wanting nothing. My love for you completes my soul, and it completes my life. Our love story covers a lifetime. Most people would read it and wonder why I needed a lifetime to fall for you. But what those people don't realize is, I didn't need a lifetime to fall in love with you. I needed a lifetime to show you just how much.

I want you to know that you made me feel so loved. You know someone truly loves you when you don't even think twice about wiping away their tears, their sweat, and even their sickness. When you would do anything to make them not hurt anymore. When you would climb into a freezing tub of cold water to hold them while you try to bring their fever down. When you would carry them from one end of the airport terminal to the other because their legs were too weak to walk. When you would trade your first class tickets in for coach just so you can sit in the last row of the airplane by the restroom in case they get sick. When you would jeopardize your career just so you could hold their hand when they felt so sick they thought they were going to die. Your love was so overwhelming, so unexpected, so life affirming. I can't imagine my life without you. If I was given the chance to live life over again, I would only choose to do so if you were in it. For me, life isn't worth living if you're not in it.

Thank you for sharing your life with me. Thank you for sharing your friends with me. During these two months away, I often found myself missing Ian and Linda, Justin and Amanda, and Sarah. We have had such great times together this past summer. I know that Ian, Sarah, and Justin are busy with filming, just like you used to be, but I know they will drop anything to be with you. Count on them. Find peace in them. Let them hold your hand. Let them embrace you. Let them wipe your tears away. Let them wipe your sickness away. Have faith in the healing power friends have to offer. Like I said before, they will never let you fall.

I want to thank you for allowing me to believe again in those long walks on the beach, sharing a bowl of ice cream, having a man wrap his arms around mine while helping me reel in a big catch, and lying next to each other on the hood of the car at the drive-in movie theater. You allowed me to believe again in a man opening the door for me and pulling my chair out for me before I sit down to eat dinner at an intimate, fancy restaurant, in kissing good night before you go to sleep, and falling asleep every night in the arms of the man that I love. You did all these things for me, and you made me believe in that one true love, but most importantly, Ryan, thank you for believing in me and all that I could give you. My grandfather used to say, "The more you laugh, the longer you live." Well, if that's the case, then I should live forever after being with you. Well, undoubtedly, I am going to be the exception to my grandfather's rule when it comes to laughter, but I certainly am not going to be the exception to my own rule of laughter: the more you laugh, the happier you'll be when you die. Thank you for providing me with endless amounts of laughter. If you didn't have your good looks, your sense of humor would certainly make up for it.

Heaven. I have often thought of this mysterious place, especially after I got sick. Is it an idea? Is it an actual place? What does it look like? What does it feel like? Is it tangible? Is it ethereal? But the more I think about it, the more I believe it is different for everyone. You are my heaven, Ryan. MY heaven.

I truly believe God started me on my journey to heaven the day I met you. Every time you smile at me. Every time you touch my face. Every time I fell asleep in your arms. These are all little pieces of my heaven. Please don't cry for me. Please know that because of you, the last two years of my life have been the most extraordinary, and I felt no pain, just love and joy. Please promise me you will return to your life, to the life that has made you who you are.

As you have helped me to find my little pieces of heaven, I can only hope I was able to help you find some of yours. My hope is that these thirty-

three letters will be pieces of your heaven. Read them over and over. Remember how much I loved you, and even though it was for a very short time, I got to experience the greatest love of all, and that completed my life.

> *Thank you for being so good to me.*
>
> *With all the love I was able to give,*
>
> *Larkin Boone*

After Ryan folded the last letter that she had written to him, he, for a moment, closed his eyes and tried to see her. Tried to feel her. Tried to smell her. The sounds of the seagulls flying overhead, the sounds of the boats passing by, the sounds of the banner-towing airplanes circling overhead had suddenly faded from Ryan's ears, and as the silence had caught his attention, he opened his eyes and saw her sitting there, smiling at him, staring at him.

"Lark…" He was captivated by her presence. "You're here," he said with relief in his voice.

"Hey, Ryan." Her voice brought peace to his mind.

He grabbed her hands. "I finished your letters. I wish there were more."

"So do I, Ryan. I wish I could have written you more."

He reached out and brushed her cheek with his fingers. "I see angels in your eyes. I don't know who I am without you. When I'm not around you, it's like I'm not with me." He paused as she played with his wedding band.

"When does it get better, Lark? Do you know when it gets better?"

"You have to let me go."

"How am I supposed to do that?"

"You need to remember that you didn't break your promise to me. You need to remember, Ryan."

"How do I do that? How do I remember?"

Larkin knelt down on the boat floor before Ryan. "Close your eyes, Ryan."

"No, Larkin. I won't do that." He knew she would be gone when he opened them.

"Ryan, close your eyes. It's okay. I am going to help you remember."

As he violently shook his head no, she placed her hands over his eyes. "Close your eyes and remember. It's okay, I'm here." As she stood up from her knees, she guided Ryan up from his seat and stood with her hand still covering his eyes and led him into a slow dance. As they swayed back and forth, Larkin began to quietly sing their song. Her voice was magical, just like when she would read to him. His lullaby had come back to him, even though it was for just a moment. And that moment was all it took for him to remember. The words she sang helped him remember what she had wanted him to.

And as he relived that memory in his mind, he could feel the touch of her hand and the sound of her voice dissolve into the autumn zephyr.

CHAPTER 13

Ian drove nervously down Atlantic Avenue as Sarah and Justin sat quietly in the passenger seats. Longport, like all the other Jersey Shore towns, was a ghost town in January. There was barely any traffic, just the occasional passing car, and there was no foot traffic. All the stores were closed for the New Year holiday except for the only gas station in town, and it was certainly too cold for anyone to be outside anyway. They had been staying in town the past two nights reluctantly awaiting the call from Ryan. The call that Larkin was dying. Ryan was their best friend, and they would do anything for him so neither of them thought twice about coming. Of course, the three of them had grown closer to Larkin over the past six months, and they had come to love her just the same.

As Ian approached the corner of Atlantic Avenue and Eleventh Avenue, red and blue flashing lights illuminated off the emergency vehicles, and the road had been blocked off, not allowing him to make the left-hand turn to get to Ryan and Larkin's house. Ian pulled over to the side of the road to call Ryan. He waited and waited as the other line rang six times. Voice mail. Ian hung up and tried again. Voice mail.

"He's not answering. I'm not sure where to go." Ian asked Sarah to keep calling Ryan while he looked around to see if there was a side road to turn onto.

"Ian, just park in the flower shop lot, and we'll walk. It's not that far. Ryan walks here every morning," Sarah said as she began to dial Ryan's number.

Six rings sounded on the other end of the call before transferring over to Ryan's voice mail. "He's not answering." Sarah left a message. "Ryan, hey. We're not able to get down your road. It's closed because of an accident or something. Ian is parking in the flower shop lot, so I guess we'll walk down to the house."

They locked up the car, and the three of them made their way across Atlantic Avenue. Ian was trying to see what all the commotion was about at the intersection where all the emergency personnel were working. A strong sense of panic was wafting through the cold winter air, and he could see the paramedics frantically working on someone. He didn't see any cars, and nothing was on fire. He wasn't quite sure what to think. As he focused his attention to Larkin and what they needed to do to help Ryan, Ian noticed Justin had stopped walking and was staring in the direction of the accident.

"Ian?" Justin called out. "Didn't Ryan tell you he was walking up here to the flower shop to get Larkin some flowers?"

"Yeah, why?" He could sense the anxiety in Justin's voice.

"Isn't it closed?"

"Yeah, but the owner opened it for Ryan," Ian explained. Ian had met Harry on a couple of occasions when he came to visit.

"So no one else would have been coming to the flower shop today?"

Ian could still sense the anxiety in Justin's voice. "Probably not. Why, Justin? Why are you asking me this?"

As Ian turned fully around to face Justin, a bouquet of flowers, cyclamens to be exact, that were laying disarrayed on the pavement just inside the police caution tape caught the corner of his eye. Ian knew cyclamens were Larkin's favorite flowers. He also saw Harry pacing back and forth outside of the caution tape with worry expressed across his face. Suddenly, his body was paralyzed with fear. He was frozen, and everything around him was spinning.

"Oh my...oh my god!" Somehow his adrenaline took over, allowing his legs to run through the caution tape, and once he got past the tape and all the personnel, his fear had been confirmed. He was suddenly thrust back by a swarm of policemen, and as he fought to release himself from their grasps, he could hear Sarah crying aloud. "Oh my god! Ryan!"

Ian pleaded with the policemen to release him. "Let me go! We're his family! Let me go!" He felt them release their grasps, and he rushed to Ryan's side as the paramedics worked on him. He was bleeding from his head and his nose, and his body was lifeless. Ian grabbed his hand. "Ryan? It's Ian. Ryan?"

Ryan opened his eyes and looked at him. "I promised Larkin…." He was barely able to speak, and as her name was whispered from his lips, he lost consciousness.

"Ryan! Open your eyes." Ian shook Ryan, trying somehow, someway, to get him to open his eyes again.

"Go, Ian. We'll stay with him. Go to her, Ian!" Sarah screamed at him. Ian hesitated, not wanting to leave his best friend's side.

"Go, Ian!" Sarah screamed again.

Justin pulled Ian aside trying to calm him down. "Ian, go! We have Ryan. Go to Larkin."

CHAPTER 14

Larkin, my dearest wife,

I read your letters. Just like you promised in your letter, you shared everything with me in them, and now, I am going to share everything with you. For the past two months, I haven't been able to talk about you and what happened. Now, I am ready, so I am going to share with you everything that has been on my mind and in my heart.

When you're dreaming with a broken heart, the hardest part is waking up. I crave your presence in my dreams. I can feel you, see you, and smell you when I dream of you. I don't want to wake up. Sometimes, I open my eyes, and I feel and see you lying next to me in my arms. You feel so real, but if I look away or close my eyes for just one second, you're gone.

Do you remember those last few days together? We had just returned from Hawaii, and you weren't doing too well. We had just made it home to Longport, just as you had wished for. It was a long travel day, and I knew you were having a hard time making it through. I carried you every step of the journey, and I held you in my arms as we sat in the back of the airplane. I wanted the trip to be as stress-free as possible for you, so we traveled overnight to avoid any crowds and unwanted advances from people who might have recognized me. I was just happy to see you were able to survive the trip.

Even though we were back home, I kept my promise to you and didn't tell anyone we were back. Just Ian, Sarah, and Justin. Just like you had asked. The hospice nurse told me it was only a matter of days, so I wanted to make sure they were in town. And as I knew they would, they made sure they were. You always knew what was best for me, Larkin. You knew I would need them here. You knew I wouldn't be able to get through it without them. Don't worry though, my lovely, as per your wishes, they kept their distance and never came to see you. You made me promise it would be only me at your side when the end was near.

I had such a hard time accepting it when the nurse told me, "Two days, maybe three if she's lucky." It was New Year's Eve night when she told me that. I couldn't help but think of the irony of the situation we were in. As a life was ending, a new year was beginning. I didn't even want to think about facing the next year without you, let alone the next day. I climbed into the bed next to you and pulled you close to me. You were in and out of consciousness as I held you, and I could feel how small you had become. It was as if death was taking bits and pieces of your body, and life was being pulled out of you with each breath you exhaled. As I lay with you, I thought about the past two years we had spent together. I remember wishing I would have given anything to have realized my love for you a long time ago. I was too consumed with my career, and the fame and the fortune had clouded my mind so I hadn't been able to see it. I am only left to wonder what you and I have missed during all the time we weren't together.

I remember feeling you stir at 2:30 a.m. I hadn't slept at all. I didn't want to miss the slightest chance you might wake up. I wanted to talk with you as much as you were able to, but more importantly, I wanted you to know I was there with you, just like I promised.

You mumbled my name, and I let you know I was there. You reached up and placed your hand on my face. I can still feel it. The magic in your fingertips. I'll never forget what you said to me. You told me I was beautiful, your beautiful-faced boy. You asked me not to turn my face away. You wanted it to be the last thing you saw.

I tried so hard to hold the tears back as my eyelids began to swell. I didn't want you to see me cry, even though you told me it was okay to cry. I smiled at you as best I could. I told you that you were beautiful and you looked like an angel. And you did, blue eyes, you looked just like an angel.

We continued to stare into each other's eyes, even though you struggled to keep yours open for more than ten seconds at a time. I would brush the falling bangs out of your eyes in between an occasional kiss on the forehead, and frequent "I love you's" filled the melancholy quietness of the air. As I felt your breaths getting shallower and shallower, I would pull you closer and press my lips against yours, trying anything I could to help you breathe easier. I asked if you were suffering, and although you tried to assure me you weren't, I was so worried that you were. It certainly seemed as if you were. Your difficulty breathing, your difficulty speaking, and your coughing had started to take its toll on me. I couldn't bear to see you like that.

I relive our next conversation over and over in my mind. You know, the one when you gave me your ring…

"Larkin, I am so sorry I couldn't save your life. I am so sorry." He could feel himself starting to lose control. He knew he was going to lose her.

She brought her hand up to his face and wiped away the tears from the corners of his eyes. "Ryan, don't do this to yourself. You gave me an amazing end to my life. You kept me alive. Without your love, I would have died a long time ago. You gave me a reason to keep living."

"I am so sorry I couldn't save your life because, Larkin, you saved mine."

"So then, keep on living. Keep on thriving. Go back to what you do best. Promise me you'll go back to acting again. Promise me, Ryan."

"I promise, Larkin. I will." He swept her bangs from her forehead.

Larkin reached for Ryan's right hand that had been resting on her cheek. "Give me your hand, Ryan. Let me see it."

He positioned his hand into hers, and he felt her place something cold and round inside of it. "Take this, Ryan. You'll always have a piece of me."

He opened his hand and saw her wedding band. He gripped it tight and wrapped his arm around her small, frail, almost lifeless body. "I will always love you, Larkin."

"I want to listen to your heartbeat. It's my favorite lullaby," she said as she buried her head underneath his chin, and he rested his hand upon her head as he felt her breathe.

He stroked her hair and rubbed her back as she drifted off into sleep. Thankfully, he could feel her breathing, so he knew she was still with him. He could only hope, only pray, that she would make it till morning so he could maybe, if he was lucky, see her blue eyes again.

...You made it through the night, but the nurse came in to check your vitals and then informed me you probably only had a few hours left. She was sorry and advised me to start making phone calls to the people who needed to know. God, Larkin, if only you could understand the pain that

was searing through my heart. I had never felt like that before. I could barely catch my breath. I scrambled back into the bedroom to grab my phone. I had been dreading this call. This phone call signaled the end. I sat next to you on the edge of the bed and leaned over to give you a kiss on the cheek. I hesitantly dialed the numbers and called Ian to let him know…

"Ryan?" Ian's voice was concerned. He knew what this phone call meant.

"Ian, it's almost time. You need to come. Are you close?"

"Yeah, very. We'll be right over."

"Alright, the nurse is here. She'll let you in. I am just going to walk up to the corner and get some flowers for her." He never missed a morning, and as long as she was still alive, he would continue to bring her flowers every morning.

"Ian? Remember, don't go upstairs to see her. I know you want to, but it's not what she wanted."

"I know, Ryan. We won't."

Ryan hung up and leaned over to kiss Larkin again. "I love you. I'll be right back."

Her eyes slowly opened, and she was able to muster a smile. "Promise?"

"I promise." He held her face in his hands for a brief moment and kissed her on the nose before he turned to leave.

...After I talked to Ian, I left to go get you some flowers. The January chill bit at my face as I walked to the corner to Harry Wakefield's flower shop. It was New Year's Day, and the shop was closed, but Harry knew I would want to come by to buy you some flowers. He insisted I still come despite the holiday.

When I came the day before, he told me he was more than happy to set aside an arrangement for you that I could pick up the next morning. Harry and I had developed a good friendship over the past six months, and he always had a different arrangement ready every morning for me to pick up. They were always ready at 8:00 a.m., right on the dot. He had told me he had missed me the last two months that you and I were away, but he knew the fact that we were back home now had meant things weren't looking so good for you.

Just like he had promised, he was waiting at the door for me. As I approached the door, he opened it and wished me a Happy New Year as he extended his arm out toward me. I accepted the handshake, wished him a Happy New Year, and thanked him for gathering together a bouquet for you. He was a good man, that Harry...

"It's no problem, Ryan. I don't consider this work. I am happy to do it for you, friend. How's the angel doing this morning?" Harry asked every morning.

Ryan hesitated. "Um...Harry, not too good, I'm afraid. This might be my last trip here."

LARKIN'S LETTERS

"I am so sorry, Ryan. It breaks my heart to see you lose the love of your life at such a young age. It's not fair. You're supposed to grow old together. You're supposed to have children together. It's not fair, Ryan. I am so sorry for you."

Ryan could tell Harry had felt sorry for him. Harry was a fifty-six-year-old divorced father of three daughters, and he had often told Ryan he could only pray his daughters would meet someone that treated them the way he had treated Larkin. He had confided in Ryan about his harsh divorce and how it had left a bitter taste in his mouth for love. He had told Ryan he could only regret he hadn't experienced a love like his and Larkin's. Ryan knew Harry understood how he felt for Larkin. He had witnessed it firsthand when he would bring Larkin into the shop with him.

"I arranged a bouquet of her favorite this morning, cyclamens. It's kind of ironic, don't you think?" Harry asked.

"What's that?" Ryan was curious.

"Cyclamens represent good-bye." Harry handed over the bouquet of white and clear shades of pink petals that sat atop a bed of heart-shaped leaves to Ryan. The petals folded back along the flower stalk, giving the flowers a light and graceful appearance.

It *was* ironic. Too ironic, he thought. "Thanks, Harry, they're beautiful. He could barely form his lips into a smile.

"Just like she is," Harry agreed. Ryan smiled, acknowledging the compliment.

Ryan was halfway through the door when he heard Harry call out for him. "Hey, Ryan. Thanks for making me believe in love again."

...Larkin, what happened next haunts me. It haunts my dreams. It haunts my conscious mind. I keep reliving that day in my mind. It's as if it happened yesterday. Do you remember that day?

The ceiling light above the bed was so blinding, it was difficult for me to keep my eyes open, but the gentle comforting graze upon my cheek beckoned me to. The pain in my head was splitting, and I felt an awful crunching in my left rib cage every time I tried to take a deep breath. I didn't understand why I was in so much pain. The hospital room curtains were so thin, it seemed as if the sun was camped right outside the window, and that, coupled with the ceiling light, was enough to make me feel as if I was floating in a tunnel of light. My body ached and cried for me to go back to sleep. I succumbed to the pain, but as I let my eyelids fall, I again felt that comforting graze upon my cheek.

And then I heard a voice. That voice. I knew that voice anywhere. That voice. Your voice. My favorite lullaby.

Your voice pleaded with me to wake up. Pleaded with me to open my eyes. But my heavy eyelids trembled as I tried desperately to open them. Your voice and your touch summoned my consciousness. I could make out the delicate curve of your cheekbone through the blurriness in my eyes, and the blue in your eyes cut through the bright light like a razor. I called out to you, and I felt you squeeze my hand as it rested at my side. You were there. You were there by my side. I tried to sit up to embrace you, but the pain in my ribs was too much for me to bear. I still couldn't understand this pain I was feeling.

You begged me to not sit up. You stroked my forehead as you helped to guide my head back down to the pillow...

"You're here! I can't believe you're here!" I reached up to touch your face. "What's going on, Lark? Why do I hurt so badly?"

"It's time to wake up, Ryan. Everything is going to be okay. I'm okay. You're going to be okay. You need to wake up."

"What are you talking about? I am awake, Larkin."

"No, Ryan, you're not."

He didn't understand what was happening. *What is going on? What is she talking about? I am awake. Why is it so bright in here? Why can't I keep my eyes open? Why does my body hurt so much?* These thoughts in his mind began to unravel, and as he tried to look at the surroundings, all he could see was her face swallowed by a tunnel of light. With every turn of his head, her face were there, looking back at him with those loving blue eyes. He started to panic.

"Larkin, what's going on? I don't understand what's happening to me."

"Ryan, it's okay. Calm down. You need to wake up, and everything will be okay. Just remember, I love you and thank you for being here with me like you promised." She bent over, held his face in her hands, and after the words "wake up" were whispered off her lips, she pressed them against his.

Ryan gasped for air as his eyes opened. He could still feel her lips against his, but he couldn't see her. The bright light was gone, and he could make out the ceiling tiles that were laid out above him. He rolled his bloodshot eyes down and could barely read the words *RN: Rachel* and *CNA: Rita* on the white board that hung on the wall across the room in front of him. He looked to his left and could see snow falling outside the double window. To his right, he could make out two figures, but their faces were too blurry for him to construct any idea of who they may be. The beeping from the IV machines and the vital signs monitor that he had been hooked up to for the past three days echoed off the white, barren walls that surrounded him.

He reached up and touched his lips, still feeling Larkin's against them. "Larkin?" He looked erratically around the room. "Where's Larkin?" He was calling out to anyone who could possibly hear him.

"Ryan. Calm down." Sarah grabbed his hand. "Ryan. It's okay."

It took a moment for him to realize it was Sarah. "Sarah? Where's Larkin? Where is she? She was just here."

"No, Ryan. No, she wasn't. You must have been dreaming."

"No! I wasn't. She was right here. I was talking to her. I touched her." His anger resonated off the walls.

"Ryan, please calm down," Sarah pleaded.

Justin approached Ryan, standing up from the chair he had been sitting in across the room and held him down as he resisted Sarah's attempts to calm him.

"Ryan. Calm down. Larkin's not here. She's gone. She's not here."

"What? What do you mean?"

Justin hesitated. "She's *gone*, Ryan. You're in the hospital. You were hit by a car crossing the street three days ago. You were on your way back from the flower shop, and a driver ran the red light and hit you. She died later that day, Ryan. She's gone. I'm sorry."

"No." He shook his head, not wanting to accept the news he had just been given. "No, you're lying, Justin. She was just here."

Justin grabbed his wrist. "Ryan," he said sternly, "I'm sorry. I am so sorry, but she is gone."

...I wanted to die, Lark. I wanted so badly to be able to go back to you, back to where we were dancing and singing. When Justin told me you were gone, grief and guilt overcame my body, and that feeling was far worse than the pain I had been feeling. I hate myself for leaving you that morning. I should have never left. I am so sorry, Larkin. I broke my promise to you that morning. I promised you I would be back. I promised you I would never leave you alone. I promised to be there till the very end. And I broke that promise to you.

I miss you so much it hurts. I miss your taste. I miss the sound of your voice. I miss the way the sunshine hits your face. I can still see your face in the shadows. I can see your reflection inside my tears. The sound of your words upon the paper on which your letters were written is the loudest thing in my head.

You came to see me twice today, and we danced together. You forgave me and assured me you weren't alone that morning. Larkin, I finally remember. When you sang to me earlier today out on the boat, I remembered. I was waiting for you in heaven. I do remember, Lark. I remember being there and seeing you. You were so beautiful. You were so healthy and happy. You weren't hurting anymore, and you smiled at me. You touched my face, and your touch was so magnificent, so magical. I couldn't even feel your fingertips. They were inside of me, and the sensation that overcame my body was ethereal. You embraced me, and I led you into a dance. I sang to you our song as we swayed together. I remember you looked into my eyes, and you told me you loved me, and you thanked me for being there with you like I had promised. Then you cradled my face in your hands and you whispered "wake up" to me, and then you kissed my lips.

Thank you. Thank you for helping me remember.

I never really knew if heaven existed. I believe in God and that He created humankind, but I never could fully grasp the concept of heaven and hell. How can you know it exists if you have never been there? How can anyone know? But now I know, Lark. I know it exists, and I know you are there. That brings me such overwhelming peace.

Ian came to see me two weeks ago, and he told me something I wish he would have told me sooner...

Ian had seen the unsealed envelope resting on the living room table.

"Ryan?" Ian had joined Ryan on the back deck that morning as he nursed his cup of coffee. "Ryan? What is this?"

Ryan immediately took notice of the envelope in Ian's hand.

"You know what they are, Ian."

"You haven't opened them yet?"

Ryan hesitated. "It's not that easy, Ian. What would you do if it was Linda?"

"I would open and read them, Ryan." Ian replied firmly. "Anything to give myself closure. Did you spread her ashes yet?"

"No," Ryan whispered back. "I'm not ready yet."

Ian sat down in the patio chair next to Ryan and placed the envelope down on the patio table that separated them.

"Ryan, you need to know something. I don't know if it will, but maybe this will help you get some sort of closure." He wavered for a moment. "That morning when she died, I was with her. I held her as she died, and the entire time, she thought I was you. She was so delirious from the morphine. She had no idea it was me. She would say, 'I love you, Ryan,' and she would keep saying it."

Ryan looked over at Ian and could tell he was struggling with reliving that moment over again.

"I made sure she didn't know it was me, and every time she would say 'I love you,' I made sure I said it back. I made sure she knew you loved her."

Ryan never broke his stare out into the inlet as Ian explained to him about that morning. It was harrowing for Ryan to listen to Ian describe Larkin's last minutes of life.

"I want you to know she died peacefully, Ryan. I don't think she was in any pain. She had a hard time breathing, but she never asked for anything. She put her hand on my face and said you were beautiful. Those were her last words."

As Ryan began to break down, Ian placed his hand on Ryan's forearm and held onto it while Ryan fought to gain control.

"I'm sorry, Ryan. I know I promised I wouldn't go see her, but I didn't know what to do. You were lying on the street, and I didn't know if you were dead or alive. I knew Sarah and Justin were with you, so I went to Larkin. I knew you didn't want her to be alone. I didn't want her to be alone."

Ryan gathered his emotions and looked over at Ian. "Thank you, Ian. Thank you for being there with her. I wouldn't have wanted anybody else."

"Ryan, read her letters. She wrote them for you to read."

...I am thankful that Ian was there with you in my place. It makes me feel a little bit better, but I am still angry at myself that it wasn't me that had been there. I never got the chance to say good-bye to you. Even though I had seen you in heaven, I didn't know that was where we were, and I didn't say good-bye then either.

I would give anything to have been able to say good-bye to you.

In your letters, you often ask me why I was so good to you. Larkin, all I did was love you. It was always like you to never assume one's kindness toward you, to never think you were worthy of love. If anyone wasn't worthy of love, it was me. I still don't know what I did to deserve someone like you. I have led a life of luxury, of fame, of fortune. I didn't always make the best decisions with regards to spending time with my family and friends, but no matter what, you were always there for me. You never not answered a late-night phone call, and you never missed any of my movie premiers. Not one. You were there for me anytime it meant something to me. You always knew what to say. You always did your best to keep me grounded. You always had a smile for me whenever I needed it. You defined friendship. You should have been the poster child for what a best friend is. So I ask you, Larkin, why were you so good to me? I can only hope I was as good to you as you were to me.

You taught me how to love with all that I am. I refer back to your letter no. 6. I did what you asked of me. I fell so in love with someone that I couldn't imagine living without her. I found love. I caught it. I held onto it. I nurtured it. And I will never let it go. I will fight as hard as I can to continue to hold on and never let go. You spoke of time in one of your letters, and you were right. Time can be timeless. At least, for me it has. I feel as if time has stopped moving since you left. I feel as if I am living inside of a broken clock, and the second hand will never start up again. I am sure this is not what you meant when you wrote about wanting time to become timeless. You meant us. You wanted our time together to have no ending. That's why you left me these letters. You left them for me to remember the important times in our life together. I have finally realized these letters are what makes time timeless, and I thank you with all my heart for that.

You were right about me needing Ian, Sarah, and Justin after you died. I guess, technically, you got what you wished for. For Ian to carry you to the gurney. The three of them have been nothing short of amazing in helping me to mourn. Justin has come to see me a couple of times since you died, and he sits with me and doesn't say a word. He just listens whenever I am ready to talk. Ian pushes me to honor your memory. And Sarah, when she comes to see me, she holds my hand as we sit on the couch in front of the fireplace watching a movie. I keep finding myself saying you were right, but I am not surprised. You were always right, and you were right about two more things. One, when Sarah does hold my hand, I do feel a little bit better. And two, the three of them will never let me fall.

Since you've died, nothing much seems to matter to me anymore. I don't read the newspaper anymore, and I don't even think I have turned the television on once. I know life is going on all around me, but I don't seem to care too much about that. All I want to do is remember you, remember us, but I can feel you slowly slipping away from my mind's grasp. I am starting to forget how you feel, how you smell. I am starting to forget the sound of your voice. My lullaby.

I pray every night you will come to me so I can remember all these things, but I know I need to let you go. It would be so much easier if I truly knew you were okay. I wish I could see you were okay.

As I try to let your ghost go, please don't think I am forgetting you or that I will stop loving you. Please don't think I don't miss you anymore or that I will never think of you. That is unthinkable. Not a minute of my day goes by that I am not thinking of you. I want you to know that from here on out, everything I do, I am doing for you. Every decision I make, every accomplishment I may achieve is all for you. I want you to know I will never leave our home. I am going to stay in Longport and honor your memory to the best of my ability. Even though you are gone, I will continue to be as good to you as I possibly can be.

My dearest Larkin, thank you for loving me. Thank you for giving me something to live for. I don't know how I am going to live without your smile, without your touch, without your smell, without your lullaby. But I know I will somehow find a way. You may be gone, but I know you are now my guardian angel. I know you are with me wherever I go, and as long as I know that, I will have the strength to face anything. Knowing you loved me, I feel as if I could live on forever.

Thank you for being so good to me, blue eyes.

All my love, your husband, Ryan

The sun was setting just below the Longport Bridge that sat in the distance from Ryan's bedroom balcony. He sealed the letter inside a white envelope and penned "My dearest Larkin" on the front. He felt a sense of freedom after he sealed the envelope closed, but he still felt as if something needed to be found.

Ryan was scared her ghost would no longer come to him. He was afraid that if he moved on, she wouldn't want to come back. She wasn't real. She was just a ghost, and he understood that, but she seemed so real to him. He could feel and smell her when she came, and she gave him an overwhelming sense of peace.

He entered back into the bedroom, closing the French doors behind him. It was 6:45 p.m. It had been only four hours since he had seen Larkin on the boat, and he already longed for her to come back to him. He placed the envelope in the nightstand drawer. *Tomorrow*, he thought to himself. *I'll take care of that tomorrow.* He sat on the edge of the bed thinking about the past twenty-four hours and what her letters had meant to him, and as he tried to absorb everything she had written, he felt a gentle caress upon his knee.

Larkin.

Turning to look, all he could focus on was her smile. Her smile was brighter than the sunset, and her touch upon his knee was warmer than the sun. He wrapped his hand around hers and smiled at her for a long while.

"Lie down with me?" she asked.

"Of course," he replied, guiding her into his arms as they tangled themselves together on the bed.

"Thank you for the dances earlier today." He smiled at her. She just buried her head in his chest. He could feel her crying.

"Lark? What is it? Why are you crying?"

"Because you're suffering, Ryan. I can't bear to see you suffer anymore."

"I'm trying, Larkin. I'm trying to let you go. I need to know you're okay."

"I am okay, Ryan. I'm at peace. I am happy. Heaven is everything I ever wanted it to be."

He could hear her telling him she was okay, but it wasn't good enough. He needed to see it. "I need to see that you are okay, Larkin. I want to be there with you to take care of you."

She unburied her head from his chest and looked up into his watery eyes. "But you are there, Ryan. You're with me every minute, every second. You never leave me." She tried desperately to assure him.

"How, Larkin? How can I be there with you when I am here, alive and well?"

"Trust me, Ryan. Just trust me." She moved her body up so her face was level with his. "I was right. Heaven is different for everyone. It is what I want it to be. It is everything that makes me happy. It's amazing, Ryan. Do you trust me?" She pressed her lips against his.

"Yes," he responded.

"Good." She smiled at him. "Will you come meet me by the dune when the sun sets?"

"Yes, of course I will."

She covered his eyes before kissing him again, and as he tried to put his hand over hers, it was no longer there.

CHAPTER 15

The wind was unforgiving, and the sand whipped up from the dunes like a tornado. The wind was supposed to be breaking soon. The sky was gray and haunted by Larkin's ghost, and her ghost had taken the place of the love he had lost. Just like the wind, Ryan hadn't been able to forgive himself for breaking his vow, his promise, to her. He had promised he would never leave her alone, and that's exactly what he did. He had promised her he would be back that morning. He had seen her when he was lying in that hospital bed. She told him everything was going to be okay. She had forgiven him. He knew and understood that. Her ghost was real. He couldn't see her, but he could feel her with every gust of the wind, with every raindrop that fell upon his skin. She had been leaving signs for him so he could remember, so he could move on. The manuscript and the incomplete screenplay in the nightstand drawer, the watch she had given him many years ago that mysteriously showed up in the drawer, the CD she had left in the broken stereo that would randomly start playing their favorite song, and the flowers she had Harry deliver every morning to him just like he had done for her. These were all signs. Her ghost was an angel, and she had been there the whole time trying to guide him to remember. He realized these letters were her wings, and they were going to be his strength from here on out. Her wings had carried him to this place, to these dunes so he could spread her ashes.

Larkin's parents had given him her ashes after the memorial service, and the two of them had previously discussed where she wanted them spread. She wanted to be close to him, close to their home, and she had asked him to spread them with the wind blowing off the dunes on their private beach where they sat many times feeding the seagulls. It was that same day when Ian had given him her letters. She had the hospice nurse mail them to Ian when they got home from Hawaii.

Ryan remembered her memorial service and how everyone came to him to tell him how sorry they were and how nice the service was. He knew everyone was just trying to be nice and respectful, but he hadn't wanted to hear it. It was the worst when people would say to him, "She's with your father now." It angered him to hear that. She was supposed to be alive and with him, not dead and with his father. The memorial service wasn't nice, he thought. It was sad and unbearable. It was depressing and heartbreaking. When people got up to speak about Larkin and share their memories of her, he couldn't even look at them. He just looked down at the floor the entire time as his mother and

Sarah held his hands. He was still in pain from the accident, and the pain in his ribs was agonizing as he tried to hold back from crying. When it was Ian's turn to give his eulogy, he couldn't even tolerate to sit and listen to him as he spoke of the love between her and Ryan. He abruptly stood up from his chair and rushed to the bathroom. The pain in his ribs was even worse as he fell to his knees in front of the toilet, vomiting away his grief and guilt. Justin had come in to check on him, but Ryan had refused to come out until everyone left the service. And Justin had sat with him until he was ready.

In the past eighteen months, Larkin had been writing to him, telling him everything about her thoughts and feelings, and he never knew it. Her letters left him memories he could hold onto and relive anytime he missed her. And it was the best gift she could have given him. It just took him a while to realize it.

He wanted to give her what she had given him. He wanted her to know everything, everything he had been thinking and feeling. What he was about to do was the only way he knew how to do that.

The wind was starting to calm, and Ryan looked out toward the empty bay. There was a high-wind advisory warning boats to stay off the water. It was appropriate, he thought. Just like two days ago, when he came here to read her first letter. He didn't want anyone else around. She had asked him to come meet her when the sun set, and all he could do was pray she would come.

The seagulls were happy to see their old friend again. With each toss of the bread, their cries of thanks proved comforting for Ryan. He soaked in the surroundings. The sun was getting heavy, and as he watched the sunset, he noticed the rays that were resting just above the horizon were slowly transforming the gray skies into a heavenly pink oasis. He noticed Lou next door strapping down his patio furniture, making sure they didn't become the wind's next casualties, and Alice two doors down, giving a last minute drink to her shrubs before the sun completely set. He could see people across the inlet on the Ocean City beaches, packing up their belongings after a day on the beach, and he could see the traffic building on the Longport Bridge as the weekend tourists were beginning their reluctant voyages home. All around him, life was happening, and it had been happening since Larkin died, but he had been an unwilling participant.

His attention was diverted as the cries of the seagulls had been replaced with cries of laughter and fireworks exploding off in the distant twilight. He looked just past the dunes where he was sitting, and he noticed a few old friends down by the water. He couldn't help but chuckle to himself when he saw Sarah pushing Justin around after he playfully tackled her after scoring a touchdown in their makeshift end zone. Ryan smiled to himself as he watched Linda give Ian a peck on the cheek, congratulating him on his touchdown pass to Sarah.

And then he saw her.

Larkin had walked out from behind Ian and Linda, and she gracefully turned to look at him. She stopped for a moment as her eyes connected with his, and he couldn't help but smile at her. She was more beautiful than he remembered, and her smile had assured him she was happy. Her smile had changed his world. Seeing her happy and healthy and smiling and laughing with friends was everything he had been needing to see. As they stared into each other's eyes, he never once let his smile falter. He wanted her to know he was going to be okay.

He watched as Ian, Linda, and Amanda ran down the beach to join Sarah and Justin as they continued to playfully bicker over her touchdown, and then he quickly reverted his attention back to Larkin. She was still looking at him, but she wasn't alone this time. He was there with her. He wrapped his arm around her shoulders, kissed her on the side of the head, and guided her into a jog down the beach to join their friends. As he watched himself run toward Sarah and pick her up over his shoulder, he noticed Larkin look back at him laughing. He couldn't help but laugh back at her. She smiled one last smile at him, kissed her fingers as she brought them to her lips, and then she waved to him with a nod letting him know she was happy. He nodded back at her before bringing his fingers to his lips, and after he waved back, he watched her laugh as Ian and Justin picked her up and carried her toward the others, spinning her around and around before the seven of them finally faded into the wind.

She was finally on her own private island, an island where sickness and pain didn't exist. Only strength, love, and friendship. An island where the seven of them play endless games of two-hand touch football and dance underneath the fireworks. She was in heaven. She was in her heaven.

Ryan pulled the letter he had written to her out of his sweatshirt pocket and walked down to the bonfire pit. The pit had provided them with so many nighttime fires when they would sit out on the beach for hours every night, sometimes alone, sometimes with their friends and family. He studied the sealed letter for a while, and he would find himself occasionally looking down the beach to see if he could see her again. To see if he could see them again. But he knew. He knew the wave and the nod she had given him had symbolized good-bye. He knew he wasn't going to see her again. That was the good-bye he needed. That good-bye was his closure.

After he finished burning the letter he had written to her, he gathered its leftover ashes together and poured them into her urn.

"I'm ready, Larkin. I'm finally ready. Thank you for helping me to see you, to see the truth. Thank you for leading me out of the darkness. I love you so much. I will always love you."

And just like that, as he went to release her and the letter's ashes, a gust of wind swallowed them and carried them into the atmosphere. He was sure the gust of wind was Larkin. Her ghost had come back one last time. He couldn't see her, but he could definitely feel her. And as he watched the wind take her ashes, he couldn't help but smile.

EPILOGUE

"Nice 'n' Easy" from Frank Sinatra resounded over the surround-sound from the downstairs stereo, startling Ryan from his sleep. The time, 6:45 a.m., illuminated from the alarm clock, and as Ryan reached over the nightstand to turn the lamp on, he knocked over the *Invicta*. If he hadn't truly thought the stereo randomly turning on was Larkin's way of saying good morning, he would have thrown the darn thing out into the ocean by now. As he sat up on the edge of the bed, he leaned over to pick up the watch and caught a glimpse of Larkin's letters sitting underneath her wedding band on top of the nightstand. It had been almost a week since he finished her letters, and every morning since, he would randomly choose a letter to read. This morning would be no different. He hadn't seen her since that night when he spread her ashes, and he was slowly coming to the realization he probably wasn't going to see her ever again.

Maybe it was reading the letter as the music

played in the background, or maybe it was the way the early morning rays from the April sun caught the angle of the curtain in the bedroom window, or maybe it was the angelic presence of Larkin that Ryan had sensed, but as he folded the letter closed, he cleared the blurriness from his eyes, took a deep breath, and realized Larkin's letters were indeed his little pieces of heaven. He was ready for her wings to carry him back to a normal life.

He opened the nightstand drawer and grabbed a pencil and Larkin's incomplete screenplay and sat back against the head of the bed. He slowly studied the title page and brushed the page underneath his fingertips knowing her fingertips had once grazed that same piece of paper. He knew why she had left her manuscript and the unfinished screenplay there for him. She had made him promise her he would go back to work, and this was her way of getting him to do so. God he had loved her, and his love for her was stronger now than it was before she died. Ryan felt a sense of freedom as he crumbled up the title page of the screenplay that had read *"Jillian's Touch," Screenplay by Larkin James,* and threw it toward the end of the bed. He knew the only way he was going to be able to truly move on was to honor her memory, and he finally knew exactly how he wanted to do that. He reached into the drawer to pull out a blank, white page, slipped it underneath the paper clip, and guided the pencil to the paper.

"Jillian's Touch."

Screenplay by Larkin and Ryan Boone.

Here is a sneak peek at Ryan's Letters, the sequel to Larkin's Letters. Available now at all major retailers.

RYAN'S LETTERS

CHAPTER 1

Looking back.

That's what Ryan Boone found himself doing since his wife Larkin's death. Looking back at their time together. Every day. Looking back at all the letters she left behind. He had been going through the motions of moving forward. Making everybody around him think he was okay. But he wasn't. He couldn't stop looking back.

But today, he found himself looking down. Down into the waters of the Great Egg Harbor Bay. Watching the ripples in the water move back and forth as his boat rocked slowly against the current. Watching his reflection bounce up and down in rhythm with the rocking of the boat. Watching as his reflection started to become blurry before slowly disappearing. Watching until all he could see was nothing. Complete darkness ensued.

"Don't give up." Her voice echoed off the sale water that was slowly filling his lungs. "Ryan, open your eyes. Open your eyes, Ryan." That voice. He knew that voice.

Larkin.

Could it really be her? His eyes shot open, and he saw her blue eyes glaring at him through the foggy salt water that was swallowing his body. The rip current was fiercely pulling his legs down toward the bottom of the bay, but he could feel her fighting to keep him afloat.

"Stay with me, Ryan." Her hands cupped his face, and he could see the worry in her eyes. "Please, don't give up," she pleaded. He pulled her hands away from his face and held them tight in his. He hadn't seen her since that night on the beach – the night he spread her ashes – and he was not going to let go of her this time. He held onto her as tight as he could while they kicked up toward the surface. He could see the sun's rays slice through the ocean's layers as he got closer to the top. As his head broke through the water's surface, he could feel her grasp diminish. He spun his battered body around and around, panicked, not exactly sure as to what just happened. Almost drowning has left him confused and disoriented. But the one thing he was for sure of what the she was there. He saw her. He felt her. But now she was gone. He had tried so hard to hold onto her, but she had slipped away again.

About The Author

Jax Jillian was born in Albuquerque, NM but before she turned a year old, her parents moved east to Harrisburg, PA where she was raised. After graduating high school in 1995, Jax attended La Salle University (1999, B.A., Communication), Temple University (2001, M.Ed, Sport & Recreation Administration), and Central Pennsylvania College (2005, A.A.S, Physical Therapist Assistant).

She settled in Philadelphia, PA with her husband and son before she became a writer. Jax found a passion for motion pictures at a young age when she remembers "getting lost" in films, and that passion ultimately led her down the path to writing. She loves "getting lost" in her writing and particularly loves writing heartfelt love stories with a touch of tragedy which she believes is the key to truly reaching readers.

Jax is the author of Larkin's Letters and Ryan's Letters, two contemporary romance novels that have seen early success from reviewers, with both averaging 4.8/5 stars on Amazon and Goodreads. She is currently writing her third novel and aspires to write a screenplay one day.

When not writing, she works full time as a physical therapist assistant and as a mom to her three-year-old son.

Connect with Jax

Email mailto:jaxjillian@gmail.com

Website http://jaxjill.wordpress.com/

Twitter https://twitter.com/jaxjillian

Facebook http://www.facebook.com/JaxJillian

Amazon Author Page http://amazon.com/author/jaxjillian

Goodreads
https://www.goodreads.com/author/show/7089784.Jax_Jillian

LARKIN'S LETTERS